LOUISE'S DILEMMA

LOUISE'S DILEMMA

Sarah R. Shaber

severn
House

This first world edition published 2013
in Great Britain and in the USA by
SEVERN HOUSE PUBLISHERS LTD of
19 Cedar Road, Sutton, Surrey, England, SM2 5DA.

British Library Cataloguing in Publication Data

Shaber, Sarah R. author.
  Louise's Dilemma. – (A Louise Pearlie mystery; 3)
  1. Pearlie, Louise (Fictitious character)–Fiction.
  2. United States. Office of Strategic Services–Employees–Fiction.
  3. Suspense fiction.
  I. Title II. Series
  813.6-dc23

ISBN-13: 978-0-7278-8295-0 (cased)

All Severn House titles are printed on acid-free paper.

Severn House Publishers support The Forest Stewardship Council [FSC],
the leading international forest certification organisation. All our titles that
are printed on Greenpeace-approved FSC-certified paper carry the FSC logo.

MIX
Paper from
responsible sources
FSC
www.fsc.org FSC® C013056

Typeset by Palimpsest Book Production Ltd.,
Falkirk, Stirlingshire, Scotland.
Printed and bound in Great Britain by
TJ International, Padstow, Cornwall.

In honor of Nancy and Jim Olson and the extraordinary bookstore they founded, Quail Ridge Books, in Raleigh, North Carolina.

ACKNOWLEDGEMENTS

I am always so grateful to my family for their support and encouragement of my writing. My daughter Katie is my first reader and my son Sam my expert on computer issues and social media. Steve, my husband, is my arm candy and dearest friend.

I could not write these books without the Women of Weymouth, my writing buddies, Margaret Maron, Katy Munger, Diane Chamberlain, Alexandra Sokoloff, Kathy Trochek (Mary Kay Andrews) and Bren Witchger (Brynn Bonner). Our retreats at the Weymouth Center for the Arts and Humanities are always productive, and fun!

For this particular book I relied on The Calvert County Historical Society for research I could not travel to Maryland to do myself. And many thanks to Dan Cooper and Leah Bowman for finding answers to several questions that stymied me.

I am so fortunate that Vicky Bijur is my agent and friend, and that Quail Ridge Books is my home bookstore.

ONE

W as it an 'h'? Or just a smudge? I pulled a magni-fying glass out of my desk drawer. The mark in 'St Leonard' did look something like an 'h', or 'St Leonhard', although the rest of the address was in English. *Mr Leroy Martin, near St Leonard, Maryland, United States of America*, the address read.

'I just don't know,' I said. 'It could be.'

'Obviously, we would like to know why a postcard written in English and mailed from occupied France to an American contains a German word,' the lieutenant said. 'If that's what it is.'

The message seemed harmless enough. *Dear Leroy*, I read, *I am well and working here, no need to worry. Mother is safe too. Wishing your wife Anne a happy birthday on February 13th. Your cousin, Richard Martin.*

Thousands of people living in Axis-occupied Europe used a neutral mail service through Lisbon to correspond with friends and family in Allied countries. But I could see why the censor had passed this particular postcard to OSS – the Office of Strategic Services. If the writer was French, and Richard Martin could be a French name, why would he spell 'St Leonard' as 'St Leonhard'?

Every odd or suspect piece of mail the U.S. censor inter-cepted could be an Axis coded message. Who were Leroy and Anne Martin? Who was Richard Martin? Who was 'Mother'? Was that a German spelling of 'St Leonard', and why did the writer include the date Leroy's wife's birthday? Surely the woman knew the date of her own birthday!

'I'm Art Collins, by the way,' the thin lieutenant said, extending his hand to shake mine. 'Foreign Nationalities Branch. I mean, Lieutenant Arthur Collins. I'm not used to being in the Army yet.'

Collins's uniform was brand new. I could still see the creases where his shirt had been folded over cardboard. He was quite young, attempting but failing to grow a mustache.

Most of the men at OSS were in uniform now. The Army had taken to drafting everyone in sight, including the staff of the Office of Strategic Services. After boot camp the draftees were returned to 'temporary' duty at their old stations. So now most of the men in the building wore uniforms. And got paid less! Women weren't being drafted yet, or I'd be in a WAC uniform myself and living in a barracks by now.

'The postmark,' Collins said, tapping the card, 'is from Nantes, not far from the St Nazaire submarine pens in Brittany. We can't ignore any questionable mail that comes from that area.' Collins ran his hand through his short hair and bit his lip, distracted by worry and exhaustion. Hitler's U-boat Wolf Pack was stalking Allied convoys in the North Atlantic, sinking so many transport and supply ships that our victory against Rommel in North Africa and our future European invasion plans were in serious jeopardy.

The OSS mission had shifted substantially since the early days. Instead of writing and distributing broad reports, we were now engaged in target analysis and estimates of enemy forces. OSS had reorganized appropriately.

The Research and Analysis Branch, where I'd worked since coming to Washington, was split into four desks: Europe/ Africa, Far East, USSR and Latin America. Each had an Economics, Political and Geographic Section. The Central Information Division, or Registry, where I now worked, was created as the reference library of OSS, where all classified and unclassified material was catalogued and stored. I was one of dozens of women who worked long days analyzing and indexing intelligence so that it could be accessed by generals, assistant secretaries of state and our own OSS operatives. Our vast card catalog contained two million index cards at last count. We maintained a War Room and a Reading Room for OSS staff. The Registry held thousands of intelligence documents, the best map collection in the world, almost a million maps, a library of 50,000 books on specialized subjects and countless captioned photographs.

We maintained and added new information to thousands of biographical files.

Most of our resources these days were spent acquiring and reviewing the intelligence needed to defeat the Nazi U-boat assault on our convoys in the North Atlantic.

'This could be important,' Collins said, tapping the postcard.

As if I didn't know that. Every request that passed through this office was critical, vital to the war effort, and needed to be completed yesterday! I had an inbox full of critical documents to analyze and index. Fine, I would deal with Collins's job first thing tomorrow. I was too tired right now to even focus my eyes.

After work I waited with my fellow employees, shivering in the glacial cold, for a bus. Despite wearing wool trousers, a heavy cardigan, my beloved fur-collared wool coat, a scarf wound so many times around my face that I could barely see, and heavy gloves over the fingerless mittens I wore all day every day to keep my joints warm, I still shivered. Phoebe's thermometer had read six degrees this morning. Six degrees! I'd grown up on the coast of North Carolina, and I'd never experienced these kinds of temperatures before.

Noticing my dismayed expression, a young woman in a WAC uniform and cloak spoke up. 'It's going to be a long wait,' she said. 'The streetcars still aren't running. Ice has shorted out the electric current to the rails.'

Last night I'd eaten the macaroni and cheese special at a diner nearby and waited until the crowds thinned out to catch a bus, finally boarding one an hour after dark. I'd stood up in the aisle all the way and arrived at my boarding house about eleven. I couldn't tolerate the thought of waiting that long again! It wasn't that I was afraid; I still carried the Schrade switchblade I'd been issued at the Farm, the OSS training camp outside Washington, and often practiced the close fighting techniques I'd learned there.

An icy gust of wind blew through the crowd, and we all muttered and huddled together in misery. I didn't want to walk home, damn it! I had a sudden mental picture of myself frozen solid waiting for the light to change at the corner of 'K' Street and Pennsylvania Avenue.

'I heard the Army is sending extra buses from Fort Myer, and the police are ticketing anyone driving a car without passengers,' said a man standing near me with his head scrunched deep into his coat. His breath froze into frost on his collar.

'Maybe when the Pentagon gets out,' someone else said. 'All those cars headed north, they'll have to pick people up off the slug lines, or they'll get pulled over.'

'Pentagon traffic doesn't come this way,' another voice responded. 'They use the highway bridge further south.'

A gay jingling interrupted us. Two sleds appeared, each drawn by a matched pair of Belgian horses, occupied by a crowd of bright young things headed for any fancy hotel or supper club that might be open. The horses, blowing steam from their nostrils, wore red plaid blankets and harnesses with bells. Their passengers, wrapped in blankets, held martini glasses aloft as the horses thundered by us, cheering and laughing as they went by. The sight raised all our spirits, but as soon as the bells and laughter ebbed away and the sleds turned onto 23rd Street, our collective mood crashed again.

Just as I despaired of a warm and early night, I heard a familiar jolly voice calling out to me.

'Halloo, Louise!' It was Joan Adams, my closest friend at OSS. Since I'd been promoted I had seen little of her, or of the scholar/spies who once worked on my floor.

'Over here!' Joan called out again, and I stood on my toes to see her waving at me from the back seat of an Army Jeep. 'Come on! We'll take you home!' Joan was General Donovan's secretary, which came in handy at times. I pushed my way through the crowd to the curb and stepped cautiously into the icy street.

An Army corporal at the wheel of the Jeep extended a hand to help me climb into the back seat. 'Isn't this swell!' Joan said, pulling me further into the seat beside her. The Jeep's top was up, but afforded little protection from the cold. Joan drew half of her motor blanket over my lap, and we snuggled together to combat the cold. 'General Donovan requisitioned a ride for me as long as this artic weather lasts. We'll have you home in no time.'

'Thank you,' I said. 'I was about to go back to my office and curl up on my desk to sleep, I'm so damn tired!'

'You would have frozen solid,' she said. 'They turn off the heat at nine.'

Dellaphine lifted the whistling kettle off the range and poured steaming water into the mixing bowl, quickly dissolving the Epsom salts mounded in the bottom.

I waited for the water to cool, spending the time peeling bandage tape off my fingers after stripping my mittens and gloves from my aching hands.

'Best wait longer, baby,' Dellaphine said, but I ignored her and shoved my sore fingers into the hot water, massaging the pain away. Flipping through index cards and file jackets all day every day caused more pain in my hands, arms and shoulders than anyone who'd never done it before could possibly imagine. And then there was the typing. By the end of a workweek my hands and fingers felt like they barely belonged to my body.

'Better?' Dellaphine asked.

'Much,' I said, drying my hands on a dishtowel. I'd feel even better once I got upstairs to my bedroom and applied my own home remedy.

'So how was your day?' Dellaphine asked. Which was a rhetorical question, seeing how she had no idea where I worked. Few people in Washington were free to share any information about their jobs. I was a government girl, just a file clerk, one of thousands jammed into office buildings all over the city, typing and filing endlessly. It was a miracle the city didn't slide into the Potomac from the weight of all those file cabinets!

I was different from most government girls, though. I worked for the Office of Strategic Services, America's spy agency, created after the bombing of Pearl Harbor. I had real secrets to protect. I had even more to keep my mouth shut about now that my job had changed from supervising a branch clerical office to analyzing and cataloging intelligence. This was a big career jump for me. Most of the female analysts in the Registry had college educations from places like Smith or Vassar. I had a junior college degree in business – code words for advanced secretarial studies.

'My day was the same as always,' I answered. 'Typing, filing. How was yours?'

'I queued at the Western Market all morning and ironed sheets in the afternoon,' Dellaphine said. 'I reckon my feet are sore as your hands.'

Dellaphine was Phoebe Holcombe's colored housekeeper and cook. She and Phoebe managed the boarding house on 'I' Street where I lived. 'Two Trees' had been Phoebe's home since she was a young married woman with children. Somehow she had hung on to it despite the Depression and her husband's death.

'At least when we get our ration books everyone will get their fair share without having to get up at the crack of dawn to wait in the cold all day,' I said.

Dellaphine opened the oven door, and the savory aroma of pot roast wafted into the kitchen.

'Is that beef?' I asked. 'Where did you find it?'

Dellaphine rolled her eyes. 'Mr Henry,' she said. 'He bought it out in the country over the weekend.'

Black-market beef. Purchased directly from a farm instead of through a butcher or a grocery store in town, where shortages drove up the price.

'It's supposed to be Grade A Prime. It ain't, I know grass fed beef when I see it,' Dellaphine said. 'But we be eating it anyway. I've cooked it long and slow. It should be tender enough even for Mr Henry.'

'Henry will be lucky if he doesn't wind up in jail,' Phoebe said, coming up from the basement. 'Dellaphine,' Phoebe said, 'the towels are washed, and I hung them on the clothes line near the furnace. I don't know if they'll dry any time soon, but they're clean.'

'It's been over a month, Phoebe,' I said. 'If Henry was going to get arrested they'd have come for him by now.'

In January Henry had asked Phoebe if he could borrow her car. She agreed. She didn't drive much herself and the car needed to be driven. Henry was gone a long time; he'd gone over a hundred miles away, because Joe had checked the car's odometer after he'd returned. Henry returned from wherever he went with jerry cans of gasoline packed into the trunk and the back seat. Without saying a word he'd unloaded them all and lined them up against the back wall of the garage. We didn't say anything to him either. What could we do? Clearly, he'd bought them on the black market. If we reported him to the Office of Price Administration he'd be arrested, and none of us wanted to be a part of that. I wasn't without guilt myself. I bought sugar on the black market; I couldn't learn to drink coffee or tea without it.

We just prayed that no one from the Gas Rationing Board or the Tire Allotment Committee decided to inspect Phoebe's garage. We consoled ourselves with the knowledge that we had plenty of gasoline!

The comforting warmth of the cozy old townhouse vanished as I climbed the stairs to my room. All the radiators upstairs were shut off to conserve fuel oil. For about an hour before bedtime, Phoebe, Ada and I would cheat, pulling the rug off the floor vent in the hall to allow some heat to rise from the first floor so that we could sponge off and get ready for bed. A real bath was out of the question. Which was why we didn't need Phoebe's clean towels anytime soon.

Henry Post and Joe Prager, our two men boarders, had slept downstairs in the lounge the last few nights. Their third floor attic bedroom had gotten so frigid that frost settled on their bedcovers.

I was willing to tolerate the chill for the chance to be alone and quiet for a time at the end of my workday. Thank God I had my own room. Most government girls had at least one roommate, but Phoebe wasn't in the boarding-house business for the money. She opened her home to four boarders out of patriotism, and to help keep her mind off her two sons, who were stationed with the Navy in the Pacific.

I took a couple of aspirin tablets and mixed myself a martini from the bottle of Gordon's gin I kept in my underwear drawer. Phoebe didn't allow drinking unless she suggested it, and then only downstairs. But I knew for a fact that Henry hid a bottle of bourbon in his room. And I'd caught Phoebe herself with a glass of sherry in her bedroom once.

I'd bought a record player recently, so I slid a Carter Family record out of its sleeve and set the needle gently on one of my favorite songs, 'Wildwood Flower'. I was the only one in the house who liked hillbilly music. With my own record player I could listen to Roy Acuff and Bob Wills whenever I wanted.

Sipping the martini and listening to my hillbilly music, I couldn't help but think of my parents, who would be horrified to learn that I enjoyed a cocktail almost every day. I was a bit surprised I'd taken so quickly to some of the temptations of the big city myself!

Like not going to church. And shopping. I had my own charge account at Woody's! Making enough money to save for my future. I bought fifty dollars a month in war bonds. I planned to use it after the war to finish college or get an apartment. That is, if I could keep working. All of us government girls had been hired 'for the duration'.

Last fall the government surveyed working women to see how many planned to keep working after the war. Everyone was shocked when three-quarters of the women surveyed said they intended to keep their jobs. That wouldn't be possible. Men returning from the war would need those jobs to support their families. Most women would be discharged and sent home to keep house.

I intended to be one government girl who didn't get a pink slip.

My paycheck had just gotten larger, too, now that I'd been promoted to Research Assistant. Two thousand dollars a year! Not that I didn't earn it, mind you. I'd never worked so hard

in my life, not even at my parents' fish camp when the blues
were running.

'Where's Joe?' Ada asked.

My pulse quickened. I so wished it wouldn't! My
attraction to Joe made my life so complicated. The man was
a refugee, a foreigner, and I knew nothing about him except
what he told me, and I'd already discovered much of that
was untrue. Joe was worldly, educated, and to my mind
handsome, in a dark, mature, unaffected way. I on the other
hand was a thirty-year-old widow with glasses and an
advanced secretarial degree.

'Joe called a couple of hours ago and said he'd be working
late tonight,' Phoebe said, dishing up the fragrant pot roast,
doling out roughly the same amount to each of us. Potatoes,
onions and carrots weren't scarce, so we could serve ourselves
as much of the side dishes as we wanted. I heaped butter on
my vegetables, since we still had a hoarded couple of pounds
in the refrigerator. I loathed margarine.

Dellaphine and her grown daughter Madeleine ate in the
kitchen, of course, but Phoebe made sure they had the same
portions we did.

'This is delicious pot roast,' I said, steering the conversation
away from Joe. I was afraid someone would notice me flushing
when his name was mentioned.

'Yes,' Phoebe said, 'thank you for buying this for us,
Henry.'

Henry nodded. 'Glad to do it,' he said.

Phoebe might disapprove of Henry purchasing beef on the
black market, we all did, but once it was stowed in her refrigerator
she was more than happy to cook and serve it!

'Best enjoy it while we can still get it,' Henry said. 'When
does rationing start?'

'In two weeks,' Phoebe said. 'We'll each get a little less
than two pounds of beef a week, depending on grade.'

'How does a university lecturer work late?' Ada asked,
returning the conversation to Joe. 'What is he doing?'

'Working with his students, I'm sure,' Phoebe said.

'Who needs to learn Czech anyway?' Ada asked. 'The Nazis occupy Czechoslovakia.'

'We don't know the government's plans, do we?' said Henry. 'If the Allies invade through Greece, we'll be in Eastern Europe in no time.'

I kept my mouth shut. I was the only person at the table who knew that Joe Prager wasn't teaching anyone anything, much less the Czech language, because he actually worked for the American Joint Distribution Committee, struggling to help Jews escape from Europe. The college professor story was his cover. Oh, he had an academic background – he'd been teaching Slavic literature in London when war broke out – but now he'd joined the war against Hitler, just like the rest of us. And I'd been attracted to him from the moment I'd met him, and him to me.

'Aren't you working tonight?' I asked Ada, steering the conversation away from Joe again.

Ada Herman was an accomplished clarinetist who played in the house band at the Statler Hotel. She'd taught music lessons to children until the war. Now she made more money than Henry, Joe and me combined! Bandleaders paid plenty to replace their male musicians who were drafted. Americans had jobs and cash now, and they wanted to go out at night and swing!

Ada partied most nights long after her shift ended. She was buxom, a platinum blonde from a bottle, and had plenty of beaus. She had a secret, too, a frightening one she'd confided to me months ago. One night, terrified to see a police car parked on our street, she broke down and told me she was the wife of a German Luftwaffe pilot. They'd married before the war, when he was working for a civilian airline. They'd lived happily in New York. When Hitler took power he moved to Germany to join the Luftwaffe. She refused to go with him, but was afraid to file for divorce for fear of attracting the attention of the authorities. As the wife of a German officer she might be sent to an internment camp. Ada trusted me to keep her secret, and I intended to, although I was breaking the law by doing it.

Ada shook her head. 'The Willard ballroom's dark tonight,' she said. 'No one is going out in this weather.'

Dellaphine brought in our dessert: canned peaches with a couple of tablespoons of vanilla ice cream. I was so used to going without sugar that it tasted like peach pie to me. Even Henry didn't grumble much any more.

Phoebe twirled the radio dial, but we only heard static.

'All the stations are still off the air, I guess,' she said. 'What did the evening paper say about the weather?'

'No end to freezing temperatures in sight,' Henry said. 'I can't imagine what it's like for our boys off Greenland. They're escorting our ship convoys through gales, blizzards, and ice. I don't understand how any of our ships make it to England, what with the weather and Nazi submarines.'

I knew, but couldn't say, that Nazi U-boats had sunk a troop transport and two fuel tankers last week, that most of the ships' crews had drowned amidst the chunks of ice floating in the Gulf of Greenland, and that the British had fuel oil reserves for just three more months.

We'd gathered in Phoebe's front room on the threadbare lounge suite she'd bought back before the Depression, passing the time before we could go to bed. Gloom kept us company, like a spinster great aunt who was always in mourning. What with the weather, and daily bad news from the North Atlantic, and the Allied invasion stalled in North Africa, the specter of Axis victory in this war haunted the country again.

'Can we have a fire, Phoebe?' Ada asked.

'Yes, Phoebe, can we?' I asked.

'What a good idea,' she said, and began to rise.

'You stay there,' Henry said. 'I'll fetch the wood and get it started.'

Phoebe sat back in her chair, her hands primly resting palm down on her thighs. She'd lost weight; I could see her knees jutting through the silk folds of her fringed caftan. A dowdy crochet shawl wrapped around her shoulders. A web of blue veins marred her fine hands, and her crimped hair was streaked with gray that wasn't evident when I moved in last year. She couldn't be very old – her sons were in their early twenties, and she'd married young, so she must be less than fifty. She seemed older, a relic of a distant time, when flappers danced the Charleston and millionaires lit cigars with twenty-dollar bills. So much had happened in the world during the last twenty years, most of it terrible.

Henry stacked wood on top of crumpled newspaper in the fireplace and poked a flaming match deep into the pile. The fire blazed into life, its flames leaping high.

'Wish we had some hot chocolate,' Ada said.

'Me, too,' I answered.

'If you find any chocolate bars, pick them up and we'll make some this weekend.'

Phoebe rose and went to the front window, parting the blackout curtains and looking out into the dark street. 'It's getting late,' she said, saying what we were all thinking. 'I hate to think of Joe coming home at this hour. It's frigid outside!'

'Maybe he's staying with a friend,' Ada said.

'He would have called,' I said, remembering the morning newspaper's account of two frozen bodies found sitting upright on a bus stop bench a couple of days ago. 'Is the telephone still working?'

Henry went out into the hall and picked up the telephone receiver. 'Dial tone,' he called back to us as he hung up. 'It's working.' So why didn't Joe call?

Then we heard Joe's key turn in the front door lock and we all breathed a sigh of relief.

Phoebe and I met him in the hall.

'Well, this is a nice welcome,' Joe said in his Czech accented English, which I found so appealing in spite of myself, stripping off his gloves and scarf. Ice crusted his dark beard, and when I took his hands they were so cold! Automatically, I began to rub them, then stopped when I remembered Phoebe's presence.

'We were worried about you,' Phoebe said, taking Joe's coat.

'I almost stayed with a friend, but then a taxi passed by. Naturally, the heater wasn't working.'

'I'll go hang this in the kitchen, it's warmer there,' Phoebe said, carrying Joe's coat down the hallway.

In the seconds between Phoebe turning her back to us and Henry coming out of the lounge, Joe brushed his lips against mine and whispered in my ear. 'I found a place,' he said.

TWO

My heart thrummed. Joe could only mean he'd found a place where we could be alone!

We had no privacy whatever. We worked long hours even before President Roosevelt ordered the forty-eight hour workweek for everyone who worked in a war-related capacity, which was practically everyone in the country. We lived on separate floors in a boarding house with six other people. Neither one of us could afford an apartment on our own. Phoebe was fond of both of us, but she wasn't a 'modern' woman, and wouldn't tolerate a love affair under her roof.

In short, Joe and I had had about as much physical contact as a teenage couple courting on their parents' front porch!

As much fast partying as went on in Washington these days, it still wasn't considered appropriate for a single woman, even a mature widow like myself, to have a sexual relationship outside of marriage. Not a public one, anyway.

'Joe,' Henry said, after gripping Joe's arm, a friendly gesture very unlike him, 'we built a fire in the lounge. Come get warm.'

Henry offered Joe his chair near the fire, and Phoebe brought him a shot of whiskey from her late husband's diminishing stash. Color returned to his face and hands.

'Thank you,' he said. 'You are all very kind.'

He offered no explanation for his late return. The fewer lies he told the easier it was for him to protect his cover.

I arrived at work early the next morning. Joan had picked me up in her commandeered Jeep, announcing her presence with a couple of honks and a bellow.

I'd poured myself one of the last cups of coffee from the OSS cafeteria. It contained too much chicory for my taste, but it was hot. I drank it quickly so that I wouldn't spill it on the files and papers that crowded my tiny desk, which I swear the government had commandeered from a third-grade classroom.

It was time to get to work on Lt. Collins's suspicious postcard. I slid it out of its protective cellophane sleeve.

I must have examined a hundred pieces of mail since I started my new job, and I knew the drill. First I had to verify the picture on the front of the postcard, making sure it wasn't someplace strategic that could figure into a covert message. According to the tiny caption on the back of the postcard, the image was Rodin's drawing of the Romanesque Cathedral of St. Peter and St. Paul in Nantes.

A quick check of the Encyclopedia Britannica confirmed the existence of the monastery, illustrated with the same photograph that appeared on the postcard.

The reverse was crowded with 'Richard's' message, a half dozen postage stamps hailing from Vichy France, Portugal and Great Britain, and the circular impressions of numerous postmarks and censors' stamps. The postcard appeared to have been routed properly through Thomas Cook's Post Office Box 506 in Lisbon, passed by both Nazi and British censors, until an American censor noticed the mark that might be an 'h'.

Thomas Cook Travel Agency operated an accommodation address in Lisbon so that private and family notes could be sent between residents of Allied countries and Axis occupied countries. It was expensive: about fifty cents for Thomas Cook's service, in addition to postage. Seemed a lot for just a postcard. Why hadn't 'Richard Martin' mailed a full letter?

The Nantes's postmark read January seventeenth, 1943. Nantes, occupied by the Nazis in 1940, was on the Loire River, just upstream from Saint Nazaire, the base of operations for the Kriegsmarine, the German Navy. Saint Nazaire had been firebombed and burned to the ground by the Allies on January fourteenth, just a few weeks ago. The heavily fortified U-boat submarine pens had escaped damage, their thirty-foot thick concrete walls impenetrable to Allied bombs. The

U-boat Wolf Pack couldn't be destroyed when docked in the pens, and in the open sea the submarines were impossible to locate.

Mailing a letter or postcard through Cook's neutral mail service was an expensive process, and the message seemed inadequate to the complicated process of sending it. Of course, I didn't know Leroy, Richard, or Anne, did I? Perhaps it was life and death to them. If the postcard was innocent, the sooner I finished with it the sooner the Martins would receive it so I could get back to my real job.

My main work now, and the work of most of my colleagues in the Registry, was to index the vast amount of raw intelligence OSS received so that it could be accessed quickly. We analyzed cables, telegrams, maps, charts, and other documents, and summarized the contents on detailed index cards, sometimes as many as eight per document, so that the material could be retrieved when needed. Only when index cards were completed could materials be filed.

Before Lieutenant Collins enlisted my help yesterday I'd finished typing an index card description for an intelligence document I'd reviewed. The card read:

> Report from captured personnel and material branch, giving information from captured German troops and officers about German suffering on the Russian front, about Russian hatred of the English, about the failure of the Germans to complete their only aircraft carrier, the Graf, Goering's addiction to drugs. A small Paris prison is kept for wives of industrialists; there were corpses in it! Also R. G-2. 4 pp., 2/18/43.

Our indexing system was invented by Wilmarth S. Lewis, a private scholar at Yale. Being a private scholar meant he was wealthy and could study any subject that took his fancy without having an actual position at the University. I'd seen Mr Lewis once. He was a dandy in tweeds who smoked a meerschaum pipe. According to rumor Lewis once wrote 'nothing is better reading (except a good index) than footnotes'.

Mr Lewis's life's work was collecting and publishing the

letters of Horace Walpole. In order to keep track of the thousands of letters he kept in a dedicated library on the grounds of his estate in Connecticut, he devised a filing and indexing system to help him retrieve any letter he wanted. Lewis was recruited to the Central Information Division by his friend Archibald MacLeish, the Librarian of Congress, to organize the filing system at OSS. Which is why the Office of Strategic Services, America's spy agency, had adopted a filing system based on one designed to keep order in the personal papers of Horace Walpole, an eighteenth century art collector and novelist. Walpole wrote *The Castle of Otranto*, the British gothic novel which influenced Mary Shelley's *Frankenstein*. I had never heard of Walpole before joining the OSS, and I had no plans to make his acquaintance.

My job title was Research Assistant, however, so in addition to cataloging and indexing intelligence reports, I had research duties. Which is why Lieutenant Collins requested my help with a puzzling postcard flagged by the U.S. censor's office.

I found Olga Albright hunched over one of our microfilm readers, a big grey machine with a lighted screen that would ruin your eyesight in no time. Olga was, like me, older than most government girls. She was a third generation German-American who had taught French and German at a private girls school here in Washington. Now she spent her days combing microfilmed German newspapers smuggled out of Europe by Allied spies for any hints of Nazi troop movements or casualties.

'Olga,' I said, touching her shoulder to break her concentration, 'I need your opinion on something.'

Olga looked up from an obituaries page in *Das Postes*. 'Of course, dearie,' she said, taking off her thick glasses and rubbing bloodshot eyes. 'What can I do?'

'Look at this,' I said, handing her the postcard and indicating the mark wedged between the 'n' and the 'a' in 'Leonard'. 'Do you think that's an "h"?'

'Let me see,' she said, directing her desk lamp on the card. 'Well, perhaps. I assume you are wondering if the writer is a native German speaker? That he might have written 'Leonard' as 'Leonhard' and then tried to erase it?'

'Is it possible?'

'Of course. But,' she said, peering at the postcard, 'it's not clear to me that this isn't just an ink blob, or some kind of stain.'

I agreed with her. After all, the card had gotten through the Vichy French, Portuguese, and British censors before our zealous American censor questioned it.

Joyce Curran was secretary to the Chief of our Communications Branch. She knew as much about codes and ciphers as anyone else in her office.

'What do you think?' I asked Joyce, interrupting her cataloguing the contents of a battered canvas courier bag.

Joyce took the postcard and peered at it, stopping to pull on a green eyeshade to block the glare of an overhead light. 'Well,' she said, 'it's clearly not a cipher. And as for a code, the entire postcard isn't coded. That's clear too. That leaves us with the option that just a few words are in code, and I think that's a real possibility.'

'Why?' I asked.

'Well, there's the word "Mother". It seems oddly placed here. "Mother" could well refer to a specific person, an agent, or even an operation. Then there's the date. Why include the date? This Anne person must know the date of her own birthday.'

'It bothers me that this postcard came through Box 506 in Lisbon. So far both the Allied and Axis powers have respected the neutral mail services.'

'Me, too. That counts against it being a coded message, though; the censors are trained to spot those. A true coded message would pass through a covert mailbox. Do you know who this Richard Martin is? Or the Leroy Martins?'

'No. Finding out is my next job.'

I checked the card files for Richard Martins who had attracted the attention of OSS. There was half an index file drawer full, from a plumber in New York who displayed a swastika on his truck before war was declared, to a French minor aristocrat who lived in the Statler Hotel. There was no Richard Martin whom I could identify as the writer of this postcard.

But I should be able to find our Leroy Martin, if he existed and owned a telephone, with no problem. Our telephone book collection filled three rooms.

In the phonebook for the western shore of Maryland, where St Leonard was located, I found him. *Leroy Martin, RR Box 12, St Leonard, Maryland.* I checked the map in the back of the phonebook, and saw that St Leonard was in Calvert County on the Chesapeake Bay just a few miles north of the mouth of the Patuxent River.

Okay, I'd found Leroy Martin exactly where the postcard said he'd be. So, if Richard Martin was his cousin, as the postcard stated, perhaps Leroy was a recent immigrant, or first generation, in which case he might be found in the files of the Foreign Nationalities Branch.

FNB had been inherited from the original Office of the Coordinator of Information, OSS's precursor agency. It was tasked with monitoring foreigners in the United States and recruiting them for OSS operations if possible. Covertly, it also followed Americans of various ethnic backgrounds – hyphen-ated Americans, you might call them – and their newspapers and political organizations. FNB was the only branch of OSS empowered to act within the United States, and it clashed with the FBI, whose antipathy toward foreigners and rivalry with OSS was legendary. General Donovan and J. Edgar Hoover loathed each other.

After Pearl Harbor, FNB asked all foreign nationals to voluntarily register, and thousands did.

There was no Leroy Martin listed in the index files of FNB.

Just on a hunch, I checked the files for his wife, Anne Martin, and struck pay dirt. Anne Venter Martin had voluntarily written to FNB early in 1942. She'd emigrated from South Africa in 1902 after the Boer War, arriving at the age of twelve with her grandmother. She stated in her letter that she was unsure if she should register, as she had never been naturalized, believing that her marriage in 1913 to Leroy Martin made naturalization unnecessary. She was correct. A foreign woman who married an American citizen before 1922 automatically became a citizen.

A FNB form clipped to Anne's letter stated that she had been interviewed and was of no intelligence use. At fifty-three she was considered too old, had lost her language, and had no useful contacts.

So what could I report to Collins about the Martins? I'd learned that Anne was foreign born, but now married to an American citizen. She had emigrated from South Africa in 1902 at the age of twelve. Her parents and grandmother had been dead for many years. Her husband, Leroy, was an oysterman who apparently had a French cousin. The couple lived near St Leonard on the Chesapeake Bay. The word 'Leonard' on the envelope may or may not have been spelled 'Leonhard', but it was impossible to say for sure. It was quite odd that the word 'Mother' was mentioned in the way it was, and the inclusion of Anne's birthday was even clumsier. This was all I had to tell Lieutenant Collins. I typed up a page of notes and clipped it to the cellophane sleeve containing the postcard. I'd take it by the Photographic Field Office to be photographed for our files and then deliver it to the FN Branch before I left for the evening.

'Thanks,' Collins said. 'This is enough. Since Anne Martin is foreign-born she comes under the authority of the Foreign Nationalities Branch. We can make further inquiries.'

'What are you going to do?' I asked.

'Send someone to interview the Martins,' he answered. 'I expect that this will turn out to be a postcard clumsily written in English by a French relation, but we need to follow it up, anyway.'

So ended another glamorous day spent in the files of the Oh So Secret, Oh So Social, Office of Strategic Services! Tomorrow would be just like it, and the day after that, and the day after that, until the war ended.

*   *   *

I leaned into the chill wind as I left the office and headed toward the bus stop. WWDC was back on the air today, and supposedly extra buses were running to compensate for the still sidelined streetcars. There were no buses in sight, though, but there were hundreds of cold government employees lining the sidewalk on 'E' street, in the dark, hoping to get home at a reasonable hour.

I found the corner where Joan had picked me up yesterday, but her Jeep was nowhere in sight. She must have been working late.

What I wouldn't give for a martini right now! Served somewhere warm and cozy and bright!

I heard a familiar voice call out to me, and the honk of a car horn, but it wasn't Joan. Joe pulled up to the curb in Phoebe's car and leaned out the window.

'Want a lift?' he asked, smiling.

'I am so glad to see you!' I said.

Joe hopped out of the car and went around to the other side to open the door for me. I slid in, so glad to feel the heater blasting away.

Joe returned to the driver's seat and pulled away from the curb. I felt a bit guilty as we drove past the crowd of cold commuters, but Phoebe's car was a two-seater and we couldn't possibly pick up another person.

'I'm delighted to see you,' I said, 'but what's going on?'

'I came home early,' Joe said. 'Finished my current project.'

That meant a boatload of Jewish refugees had left a neutral port in Europe, probably Lisbon, and were bound for safety somewhere else in the world. Joe looked happy and relaxed, but it wouldn't last. Soon he'd be scrounging money for escapes, travel, and ship berths again.

'I want to celebrate,' he said. 'Let's go out to eat somewhere we can talk. Is O'Donnell's all right? I know you don't like fish, but they've got lots more dishes on their menu.'

'I'd love to,' I said. 'Can I have a martini?'

'Of course. You can have two, in fact.'

I felt the crick in my neck subside. An evening alone with Joe, where we could talk for a couple of hours without worrying that someone would sense our relationship, with martinis, and heat, sounded like pure heaven.

Joe stopped at a light and turned to me, his eyes crinkling. 'Best not to be home tonight for dinner anyway,' he said.

'Why?'

'Guess what Dellaphine has fixed for dinner.'

'What?'

The light changed, and Joe changed gears, driving more slowly as we went past the White House, where the street-lamps weren't lit and government buildings were blacked out.

'Bologna casserole,' he said. 'I understand it's layered bologna and potatoes, dotted with bacon fat.'

'How awful!'

'You should have heard Dellaphine! "I never would have thought that someday I would serve such trash at Miss Phoebe's table,"' he said, mimicking Dellaphine's accent.

'I can imagine what Henry will say!' I said.

We turned into O'Donnell's Sea Grill and parked, Joe leaning out the open car door and peering at the ground so that he could see the white lines of the parking space.

Inside, the large restaurant was warm and bright behind its blackout shades. The dining room was already packed, but there was room for us at the long bar counter and the two of us slid onto stools at one end of it.

'The lady would like a martini,' Joe said to the bartender.

'With just a dash of Taylor's vermouth,' I said, 'and no olive.'

'A pint of whatever beer you've got on draft,' Joe said, 'and a menu.'

The bartender brought our drinks, and we sat at the bar sipping and chatting.

'You haven't said anything about what I told you last night when I got home,' Joe said. 'If you've changed your mind . . .'

'No,' I said, squeezing his hand, 'I haven't, of course not!' So why had my stomach cramped into a tiny ball? 'Tell me all about it.'

'A friend of mine at work, he lives on a houseboat on the

Potomac. In the channel off Maine Street, a few docks south of the Yacht Club. Every few weeks he goes into Baltimore and spends a weekend with his mother. He said I could borrow the boat when he's gone!' It was Joe's turn now to squeeze my hand. He leaned in toward me, and we almost kissed, but then the bartender slid a menu under our noses and we remembered where we were.

We collected ourselves and scanned the menu. Joe wouldn't allow me to pay for myself when we were out, and he hated it when I picked the cheapest item on a menu, so I settled on something in between.

'I'll have the oysters and Virginia ham Norfolk,' I said, 'with a beer.'

'Don't you want another martini?' Joe asked.

'Beer sounds good,' I said.

'Okay,' Joe said. 'I'll have the Virginia crab cakes with French fries and another pint of draft beer.'

The bartender went away to deliver our order to the kitchen, and Joe and I found ourselves leaning towards each other again.

'We'll have to leave the house separately,' Joe said. 'I'll go one way, and you'll have to go another.'

'You know,' I said, 'I don't think Phoebe would mind us having an affair as long as she doesn't have to admit she knows about it.'

An affair! I'd said the word out loud! Joe and I would be sleeping together. Without being engaged, without wanting to be engaged. And I wasn't even sure I wanted to remarry, ever! I felt a flood of emotion, almost a river of feeling, pour through my body, and suddenly Joe's voice seemed very far away.

'It won't be this weekend. Maybe the next. But we can go see the boat, would you like that?'

Not this weekend! Thank God. But if I wanted this so badly, why was I relieved?

I felt my body regain control of itself. 'Sure,' I said, 'I'd like to see it.'

'If it's not so frigid this weekend we'll go,' he said.

We drove home in the crisp cold moonlight and said

goodnight to each other in the hallway. Ada and Henry were still in the lounge, so we couldn't kiss. But it wouldn't be long before we would be spending the night together. Something I still could hardly imagine!

THREE

'So, Mrs Pearlie, I see that you have field experience.'

Lawrence Egbert was the Assistant Chief of CID and my boss. He was one of the few men in the Research and Analysis Division with military experience. Most were academics or civil servants. He'd been in the U.S. Naval Reserve since 1918 and was an instructor in nautical astronomy.

'Yes, sir,' I said.

Egbert referred to the file in his hand. My personnel file, I assumed. What was this all about? A new assignment? Please God, let me escape this prison built of file cabinets even for a day!

'Your case officer was Colonel Melinsky. He's given you the highest commendation. And,' he said, leafing through a few more pages, 'you've been to the Farm. And passed all tests.' He closed the file and tossed it on his desk.

'Foreign Nationalities Branch has requested that you be temporarily transferred to them, under the supervision of Lieutenant Arthur Collins,' he said, 'to investigate a suspicious communication from France to an American in Maryland. We cannot spare you. We are seriously understaffed.'

Damn it!

'But,' he said, 'so is every division of OSS. The Head of FNB assures me that he'll need you for just a few days. So consider yourself transferred.'

'Yes, sir, thank you, sir,' I said.

'You may report immediately,' he said.

I floated out of his office, passing by my desk long enough to collect my coat and pocketbook before I found my way to the Foreign Nationalities Branch.

On my way out I passed Ruth, filing, of course. I'd worked

with Ruth before. She was once a hoity toity Mt. Holyoke graduate. Now she spent her days filing like a machine. Her fingers were double-wrapped with first-aid tape.

'You look pleased,' she said.

My training kicked in. I couldn't tell her any details about my assignment. 'On an errand for Egbert,' I said. 'Might be out of the office for a couple of days. If someone asks where I am . . .?'

'I'll take care of it,' she said. 'Have fun.'

'Fun' was a completely inappropriate word to assign to an OSS assignment, but I was already enjoying myself! A break from the tedium of office work was just what I needed.

Collins offered me his chair and perched on his desk, one of a dozen squeezed into an office in a corner of the building that housed the Foreign Nationalities Branch on the OSS campus.

'Cigarette?' he asked, pulling out a packet of Luckies and holding the package out to me.

'No, thanks,' I said.

Collins extracted a cigarette from the packet with his lips and lit it, striking his match across the wood of his desk, already deeply scarred. He inhaled deeply, and I noticed his shoulders slump with relief.

'Poole wants me to interview the Martins,' Collins said. DeWitt Poole, who'd run the American intelligence network in Russia during the Bolshevik Revolution, was the head of the Foreign Nationalities Branch. 'The specificity of the date concerns him. And the address, right on the Chesapeake Bay, near the Solomons Island naval base and an air base.'

'I understand that,' I said.

Collins lowered his voice, so his officemates couldn't hear him. 'It's good that you're coming with me,' he said. 'Having a woman along to interview civilians is good intelligence practice. It puts the subjects at ease.'

If a woman accompanied Collins, in other words, the Martins wouldn't take the interview as seriously as they might otherwise.

'I've requisitioned a car,' he said. 'We need to go today. St Leonard's about a hundred miles away, and it will take us about three hours at the war speed limit, I reckon. I know my way around the western shore of Maryland, though; I vacationed there when I was a kid.'

A bitter wind swept the government parking lot, sending chewing gum wrappers and cigarette butts skittering along the pavement. Collins opened the passenger door of a two-door black Chevy sedan with government license plates. I stepped on the running board and slid inside. I was grateful it wasn't an open Jeep and appreciated the blast of heat that enveloped me once the engine started.

Getting out of Washington was not as difficult as I had expected despite the icy condition of the streets. Our tires were brand new, and chains rattling on the rear wheels gave us traction. It wasn't long before we found ourselves in rural Maryland, driving east, then south, on state roads, more or less parallel to the western shore of the Chesapeake Bay.

On the inland side of the road lay fallow tobacco fields, barns, and empty wood hogsheads waiting for spring and summer, interrupted by picturesque farmhouses and dairy barns. The fields were empty. In this cold weather livestock huddled together inside sheds and barns to keep warm.

On the beach side of the road, turn-offs were marked for the famous western shore beaches – North Beach and Chesapeake Beach. I wondered how these Maryland beaches differed from those lining the coast of North Carolina. Collins noticed me studying the signs.

'I went to the northern beaches every summer when I was a kid,' he said. 'We camped in Seaside Park for a month. To get there we caught a steamer from Baltimore. We bathed in the ocean, rode the carousel, fished from the pier. My father would fry whatever we caught over our campfire. Sometimes we'd go out to eat dinner at a crab house and then get ice cream at Forest's Ice Cream Garden. I thought it was heaven.'

Growing up in Wilmington, North Carolina I knew how

much tourists loved summers at the shore. Those summers were much less fun for the locals. Waiting on tourists was long hard work. For me, life in a big city like Washington was heaven!

'It's so different in the winter,' Collins said. 'The campgrounds, piers and dance pavilions are closed. Even during the season there's not much going on at night. Can't have too much light and sound near the Bay these days anyhow.'

'Seems a bit silly,' I said, 'all the paranoia on the coast when the war began, what with the fortifications on the Chesapeake. A Nazi canoe couldn't get through. And the Nazis don't have a single aircraft carrier.'

The Bay bristled with military bases. There was Fort Storey, Fort Custis, Camp Pendleton, Portsmouth Naval Yard, and Langley Field, all within a few miles of each other at the mouth of the Bay. They were linked to each other with gun batteries, minefields, submarine nets, search-lights, radar stations and a couple of lighthouses. Further up the Chesapeake a submarine net closed off the Rappahannock River to protect Richmond. Washington itself was circled by Fort Hunt, Fort Washington, Andrews Air Force Base, Bolling Air Force Base, Fort McNair, and the Navy Yard.

The Potomac River had its very own submarine net, though the gates were left open and the mines set on safe mode most of the time to keep our own shipping from damage.

St Leonard, where we were headed to meet the Martins, was located on a narrow peninsula bordered by the Patuxent River and the Chesapeake Bay. The Patuxent River Air Station and the Solomons Island Naval Training Base occupied the southern tip of the peninsula.

PT-boats and auxiliary Coast Guard cutters patrolled the Bay and the rivers – when they weren't blocked by ice, that is. And the Coast Guard patrolled the beaches. The place was safe as could be.

The state road became Solomons Island Road before we got to St Leonard, a picturesque town a couple of miles from the coast.

'We should get lunch before we find the Martins,' Collins said. 'It's about that time.'

We parked in front of a shingled building that, according to the directory posted outside the main entrance, housed a general store, the post office, a library and Bertie Woods' Cafe.

The lunchroom, decorated with crab pots, nets hanging on the wall and faux captain's chairs, was packed with the lunch crowd, mostly men in work clothes. We were able to find an empty table for two next to the kitchen. That was okay with me; it was warmer there.

Our waitress filled our water glasses and handed each of us a menu, a single sheet with seven handwritten items, three of which were beef. Of course, we were out in the country. Beef was easier to come by.

'You're very busy,' Collins said to the waitress.

'Been that way since the war started,' the waitress said. 'We used to close in the winter, after the tourists left. Now the boarding houses are full of people working at the naval training station, and they got to eat.'

I ordered a hot roast beef sandwich and milk. Collins had pork chops with corn and mashed potatoes. He requested a beer too, which bothered me, since we were working.

When the waitress returned with our drinks, Collins drained half his beer in one gulp. When he noticed my disapproval, he looked flustered for a second, then shrugged. 'This is just a routine interview,' he said. 'No reason I can't have one beer.'

If there was one thing I'd picked up at OSS, it was that an agent – and we were agents, even though this was a small matter – should be ready for any situation. Alcohol just wasn't good preparation. But I couldn't say anything to the man in public.

'Listen,' Collins said, after another swig, 'when the waitress comes back, I'm going to ask her where the Martins live.'

'What's our cover story?'

'Surely we don't need one. I'm just asking directions.'

'But we can't just—'

The waitress arrived with our order.

'Thank you,' Collins said as she set down our plates. 'Do you have a second for me to ask you a question?'

'Sure,' she said.

'Can you give us directions to the Martins' place? Anne and Leroy Martin? Do you know them?'

The waitress crossed her arms, and a suspicious look crossed her face. 'What do you want with them?' She surveyed Collins's uniform and my tailored wool dress. 'Are you from the government?'

'Yes,' Collins answered easily, and I don't think my imagination was playing tricks when I sensed a lull in the conversations at the tables around us.

'What part of the government?' she asked.

Collins hesitated, and the ambient noise from the lunchroom rose in volume. Goddamn the man!

'We're from the Office of Price Administration,' he said. 'Mr Martin has applied for permission to purchase two new tires. We're here to inspect the tires he owns now. That's all.'

A burly man in a ragged fisherman's sweater stood up from a nearby table and almost kicked his chair aside as he moved towards us. 'Is that nice shiny car outside yours?' he asked. 'The Chevy with the government plates? The one with four tires that actually got tread? Ain't it something that we got to beg the government for new tires that we can buy with our own money and you drove all the way out here on four new ones!'

I waited for Collins to reply, but he looked unsure of himself, and I noticed that his hands, resting on the tablecloth, trembled slightly.

'Sir,' I said to the angry man, 'we don't have anything to do with the car. We got it from a motor pool. We're just doing our jobs.'

'It takes two people to check Leroy Martin's tires? And you come a hundred miles to do it!' he said. 'If we win this goddamned war it will be a miracle!'

The man turned his gaze on Collins. 'And you!' he said. 'You're in an officer's uniform! Why aren't you fighting? My older boy's just a buck private in North Africa, and I ain't got a letter from him in two weeks. I don't know if he's alive or dead!'

'Come on, Dennis,' the waitress said. 'Forget it.'

'Yeah,' another man from his table said. 'These two aren't the enemy. Finish your coffee. We're due back at work.'

Collins and I finished our meal hurriedly, paid our bill and left the lunchroom, not without receiving more critical stares from the patrons.

Once outside Collins stopped by the car to light a cigarette. 'We still need to get directions,' he said, inhaling deeply. 'Thanks to that hick.'

'Let's get inside the car,' I said, trying not to sound furious.

'But—'

'We should not be having this conversation where someone could overhear it!'

'All right, all right.'

Once in the car, I turned to him. 'What was that about?' I said. 'You've made a mess of this! Gotten the attention of the entire town, and not good attention. This is what happens when you're not prepared!'

He recoiled at my intensity. 'What are you talking about? Those are just a bunch of rubes. We can get directions from someone else, at the filling station maybe . . .'

'You've invented a cover story that makes no sense! What are we going to do when we get to the Martins? Ask to see their tires, then say, "By the way, there's this postcard!"'

'Okay, Miss Secret Agent, what would you do?'

'You find one person, ask them for directions innocently, don't call attention to yourself, don't make up some story that will fall apart later!'

'Okay, you do it if you're such an expert!'

'Just drive!'

'Where?'

'Down the street a ways.'

We had to wait for a military convoy, mostly Jeeps and a couple of trucks, their cargo covered with khaki canvas, to pass before we could turn out of the post office parking lot.

A few blocks later I spotted an older man with a cane walking his dog.

I told Collins to stop, rolled down my window and spoke to the man. 'Sir,' I said, 'can you help us?'

'I'll try, young lady,' he answered, tugging on the dog's leash to bring him to a halt. The aging collie, his nose thick with white hairs, obediently sat down on the cold ground and leaned his head against his master's knee to be scratched.

'We're in town to see Leroy Martin – his wife is named Anne? And I think I've missed the turn. Their place is right on the Bay.'

'No problem at all,' he said. 'Go south on this road here, Solomons Island Road, for a piece; you'll come to the turnoffs for Long Beach and Calvert Beach on the left. Pass those on by, and soon you'll see the Martins' mailbox on your left. Turn there. It's just a dirt road, easy to miss. If you see the sign for Flag Ponds you're near the bluffs and you've missed it.'

A mile down the road Collins spoke. 'I don't see how asking that guy for directions was so different from what I did in the restaurant,' he said.

God, I was working with an imbecile!

'Have you done anything like this before?' I asked.

Collins compressed his lips. I could see he was angry.

'Okay,' he said. 'No, I haven't. I've been manning a desk since I got to OSS. I haven't even been to the Farm yet. We're so short of manpower, I got assigned to do this because there was no one else. Happy now?'

'When we get there, let me handle the interview.'

I could see Collins's jaw clench. I didn't care. I'd been pulled away from my desk job to back up an inexperienced officer because I had some field experience. It was up to me to salvage this visit if I could.

'All right,' he said, surprising me. 'But I write the report.'

'Sure,' I said. Of course Collins would write the report. He was the man in charge.

We found the turn off to the Martins and made our way down the rough track paved with gravel and crushed oyster shells. A half a mile from the main road we crossed over a stream on a wooden bridge. The track meandered for over a mile longer alongside a dense stand of white cedars, finally ending at an oysterman's cottage in a clearing. The track, which I suppose you could consider the Martins' driveway, divided the cottage from the woods and a wide, deep inlet.

The Martins' cottage was a weather-beaten grey, which I suspected had faded from blue, with fresh, bright, white painted trim. More crushed oyster shells paved the walkway to the front door and to the head of the pier on the inlet just yards from the house. A skipjack was moored there, frozen in place by ice. The oysterman's boat was winter proofed, its sails furled and deck covered with canvas secured with rope. Old tires were roped to the side of the pier, which kept the skipjack from crashing against it.

Ice coated the rocks that lined the shore and extended several yards out into the water, despite the lapping of tiny waves on the beach. The Chesapeake Bay was an estuary, which meant that it had tides, but even a surging tide couldn't prevent the buildup of ice on the shoreline in these temperatures.

Patches of wispy Chesapeake Bay fog, which formed when moisture from the Bay collided with crisp air blowing in from the west, floated through the clearing, sometimes obscuring the cottage or the inlet before drifting away. A couple of miles south along the coast the beam of light from the Cove Point lighthouse reached out to sea.

A fish eagle perched on a tree limb near the head of the pier. At first I thought it was frozen solid, it was so still. But then it heard our footsteps, and after flapping its wings a few times and hopping about, it flew off. If a bird could fly stiffly, that osprey did. I wondered how birds and other wildlife could survive in this cold.

*   *   *

Collins knocked on the front door of the cottage. We heard light footsteps, and then the door opened.

The woman must have been a beauty when she was young, and she was still handsome. She had a good figure on a sturdy frame. She wore a simple deep-green wool dress and a perfectly pressed and starched apron. A full head of wavy light-brown hair dropped to her shoulders. Her skin was exquisite, not a line on it, and she had color in her high cheekbones. I knew she was in her early fifties, but she didn't look it.

'Can I help you?' she asked.

'Is this the home of Leroy and Anne Martin?' I asked.

'Yes, it is,' she said. Then she took in Collins's uniform, and a look of uneasiness crossed her face.

'Is something wrong?' she asked.

'Not at all,' Collins said. 'Can we come in?'

'Of course,' she said. 'We're just finishing lunch. My husband's shift starts at three.'

We entered a small front entryway that was used mostly for storage. It contained a coat rack hung with foul-weather gear and a bench lined with rubber boots. We crossed through it into a tiny, warm kitchen and then into a back room which ran the length of the house. Windows lined the back wall, giving a stunning view of the Bay. Several birdfeeders stood outside, crowded with nuthatches, orioles and cardinals.

Leroy Martin rose from the round table where the two of them had been eating lunch.

Unlike his wife, Martin's face was dark and deeply lined from years in the sun. His hands were rough with callouses.

'You're from the government,' he said. 'What do you want?'

'Come sit down,' his wife said.

'They're not staying long enough,' Leroy answered.

There appeared to be some hostility to the government around these parts, I thought.

'They can still sit down,' Anne said.

So we sat on the couch.

'We're from the Office—' Collins began.

'The government,' I interrupted. 'The censor's office flagged a postcard addressed to you, Mr Martin, that we want to ask you a few questions about. It's from France.'

'France?' Leroy said, still standing, his arms crossed across his chest. 'We don't know anyone in France. Do we?' He looked at his wife, who'd taken a chair near us.

'No,' she said, straightening her apron over her knees. 'Not that I can think of.'

'You're originally from South Africa, I believe?' Collins asked her.

'Yes,' she said, 'but I've been here since I was a child.'

'You let me handle this,' her husband said. Anne fell silent, but she didn't seem to be afraid of her husband. 'My wife is an American citizen,' Leroy said. 'She has no connections overseas at all.'

'It's addressed to you,' I said. 'Just take a look at it, please. It seems to be from a relative of yours, Mr Martin.' I handed him the cellophane sleeve, and he inspected the postcard.

'This is loony,' he said. 'I don't have kin in France, and I don't know any bloody Richard Martin. This must be a mistake of some kind, or a joke.' He handed the postcard to his wife to read.

'Where is your family from originally?' Collins asked.

'What are you implying?' Leroy asked. 'That I ain't an American? If you weren't wearing that uniform I'd beat you into the ground!'

'Mr Martin,' I said, 'we're not implying anything at all. We're just trying to understand why you'd be getting a postcard from France, that's all.'

'Leroy—' Anne began.

'I told you to let me handle this,' Leroy said.

Unruffled, Anne continued. 'What about that man who showed up, before the war, and said he was your cousin? He was from France, wasn't he?'

'Oh,' Leroy said, finally sitting down, 'him. Yeah. I forgot him.'

'Wasn't his name Richard?' Anne asked.

'Yeah, it was. I'm sorry,' he said to us, 'I didn't remember.

My grandfather was French Canadian, he came here to work
the oyster beds and stayed. This Richard Martin guy was a
merchant mariner. His ship was docked on the Potomac
River for a few days, and he came over and said he was my
cousin.'

'Was he?' I asked.

'Yeah, when he went over the family stuff it made sense.
We were distant cousins though. I forgot all about him.'

'Why would he send you a postcard telling you he was
okay?'

'I got no idea,' Leroy said. 'I don't give a good god damn
if he's okay or not, I just met the man once.'

'Do you know his mother?' I asked.

'No, of course not!' he said.

'Dear, he talked about his mother while he was here. He
said she was your father's third cousin.'

'He did? If you say so. I need to go to work. You need to
be on your way too,' he said to us.

'February thirteenth is your birthday, isn't it?' I asked
Anne.

'Yes it is. I was born in 1890,' she said.

'You don't have to answer any more questions,' Leroy said
to her. 'We ain't done anything wrong. I'm going,' he said,
stomping through the kitchen toward the door.

We could hear him in the entry room pulling on his coat
and boots before slamming the door on his way outside.

'I apologize for my husband,' Anne said. 'He seems brusque,
I know, but he has little patience for anything other than his
own business. It's just his way. Excuse me, I have to get
something out of the oven,' she said. 'Would you like some
tea? I could put the kettle on.'

'I don't—' Collins began.

'If it's not too much trouble, that would be lovely,' I said.
With her irritable husband out of the way, perhaps Anne
could tell us more about Richard Martin and his mysterious
mother.

Collins leaned back onto the sofa, crossing his legs and
looking resigned.

When Anne opened the oven door, the most wonderful odor

of cinnamon and apples drifted into the sitting room, but what she removed from the oven looked like no apple pie I'd ever seen before. It resembled a loaf of bread.

A few minutes later Anne brought us our hot tea on a tray, with milk and sugar.

'I hope you like it strong,' she said, pouring us each a cup and passing around the sugar and milk.

'Whatever you've baked smells wonderful,' I said.

'It's stollen, a sweetbread with nuts and fruit. The only thing that does remain from my life in South Africa is my grandmother's cookbook. I bake from it whenever I can find the ingredients.'

'Can I ask why you emigrated?' I said.

'The Bocr War,' she said, but didn't elaborate.

I set down my cup. 'I'm curious about just one more thing,' I said. 'Why do you think Richard Martin mentioned the date of your birthday?'

She shrugged. 'When he visited it was right after my birthday. In fact I think I served him leftover cake. Perhaps he just wanted to let me know he remembered it.'

Anne Martin walked us to her door and we made standard goodbyes, but then she held out her hand, palm up. When we didn't respond, she said, 'The postcard. I believe it belongs to us?'

'Of course it does,' I said, handing it to her.

She tucked it into her apron pocket and closed the door behind us as we left.

'Why did you give her the postcard!' Collins said, after we'd gotten back into the government car. 'That was stupid!'

I bit my lip, waiting until my urge to speak sharply to him passed. 'It would have looked suspicious if I hadn't, wouldn't it? If the postcard isn't innocent, now they'll think we're satisfied with their explanation. Besides, I took photographs of it back at OSS.'

Collins changed gears badly and swore at the grinding noise. 'What a place to live, especially in the winter!' he said. 'It's so isolated! We're only a couple of miles from St Leonard but it feels like the off end of nowhere.'

We regained the state road and started back towards Washington.

'We need gas,' Collins said. 'Let's stop at the filling station in St Leonard.'

I weighed whether or not to speak. 'We should stop at the next town over,' I said. 'We don't want the folks in this town to notice us again.'

He didn't answer me, but we drove past the St Leonard filling station. In fact we didn't speak until he asked me what I wanted on my hot dog when we stopped at a hot dog stand before we crossed the Anacostia River into Washington.

I was fine not talking to Collins. I resented being asked to babysit him without even being told that's what I was doing, but at the same time I was glad I was with there to run the conversation with the Martins.

I was sure Collins's report would say that the postcard was harmless, and that the Martins had explained its content adequately. I wasn't so sure. The reference to 'Mother' still worried me. Why would Richard Martin mention his mother in such a pointed way to people who had never met her, and whom he had only met himself once?

And it seemed to me that the Martins, and more than a few people in the lunchroom, weren't exactly New Dealers.

I asked Collins to drop me off on a corner a couple of blocks from home so I could walk the rest of the way. I didn't want anyone in my boarding house to see me in a government car with an Army lieutenant and ask me a bunch of questions I couldn't answer.

Joe opened the door when he heard my key in the lock.

'Good lord!' he said. 'You didn't walk all the way home from work!'

'No,' I said, 'a friend dropped me off on the corner.'

He cupped my face in his hands. I was so numb from the cold that I could barely feel them.

'You're frozen,' he said. 'Come into the sitting room. We've got a fire.'

He helped me take off my coat, and I unwound the scarf

from my neck. The heat from the fire felt wonderful on my legs.

'How was your day?' Joe asked.

'Same as always,' I answered.

FOUR

'Back so soon?' Ruth asked as I passed her file cart on the way to my desk.

'Yes,' I said, 'it was a small errand.' And although I was glad to be done with Collins, I dreaded seeing what had accumulated in my inbox during the day that I was gone.

It was stacked high, of course. There were two documents to read, index, and catalog and several research requests that needed to be completed. I settled in to work, ready to put in a very long day. I didn't want to come in on Saturday if I could help it. I'd promised Joe I'd go see the houseboat. Just thinking about Joe and that houseboat made the heat rise in my face! I angled my chair so that I faced the wall. Desperate as I was to spend time alone with him, I was grateful that I still had more than a week to get used to the idea.

A Negro messenger tapped me on the shoulder, startling me. 'Mrs Pearlie?'

'Yes?' I said.

'Ma'am, Mr Egbert would like to see you. Right away.'

'Thank you,' I said. What now?

My boss, Lawrence Egbert, wasn't alone in his office. Collins's boss, DeWitt Poole, head of the Foreign Nationalities branch, was with him.

I put up my guard immediately. What had Collins told them? Had he tried to blame me for the mistakes he'd made yesterday?

I sat down in a desk chair in front of the two men, determined to protect myself. I was not going to take the blame for anything Collins said or did! I didn't care if I *was* a file clerk, and therefore expendable.

'We have Lieutenant Collins's report here, Mrs Pearlie,' Poole said, 'and I'd like to ask you your opinion of his conclusions.'

'Of course,' I said. Poole handed me the report, and I read it quickly. It was only a page. He didn't mention me at all!

And the report was so terse that it just barely covered the facts of the day we spent in St Leonard. Collins had done his best to avoid admitting his mistakes.

Egbert folded his arms. 'What did you think of Lieutenant Collins's handling of this inquiry, Mrs Pearlie?'

I took a deep breath. I was not going to cover up for him. 'Lieutenant Collins didn't have a cover story prepared. He had a beer with lunch. He seemed to lack training on how to proceed in the field. But his questioning of the Martins was suitable and elicited the information we needed.'

Poole nodded in agreement, thank God!

'I have to accept some responsibility for Lieutenant Collins,' Poole said. 'We are so short handed. Do you agree that the postcard mailed to the Martins wasn't a covert message?'

I hesitated. I didn't want to incriminate the Martins if they weren't guilty of anything, but then again . . .

'I don't think the questions we have about the postcard were adequately resolved,' I said. 'The Martins appeared to barely know the sender, Richard Martin, and the wording of the postcard still concerns me. Why the emphasis on "Mother"? The Martins didn't know Richard Martin's mother. And why is Anne's birthday date mentioned in such a clumsy way? It could be simply that the writer wasn't corresponding in his native tongue, but still, it puzzles me.'

Poole nodded. 'I agree,' he said. 'But we have had an unfortunate complication. Apparently, Collins's behavior in St Leonard caused a commotion, and someone complained to the Office of Price Controls, which was Collins's improvised cover. The OPA called the FBI, since they'd never heard of Collins. The FBI maintains a list of our employees, and now the FBI has wind of our inquiry. As you know, the Hatch Act gives the FBI the authority to search for spies inside the United States. They have assigned an agent to investigate this postcard and the Martins.'

'Of course the Foreign Nationalities Branch would like to keep tabs on the FBI in case the agent discovers something. Otherwise we might never know,' I said, agreeing with him. My own limited experience with the FBI had been less than favorable. Hoover wouldn't share intelligence with the OSS if he could avoid it.

'We'd like you to act as OSS liaison with the FBI agent assigned to this case,' Poole said. 'Mr Egbert has agreed to release you from your current assignment as long as necessary.'

I'd been around OSS long enough to know I shouldn't be too flattered. I was just a file clerk. I'd shown I was observant, and I had some field expertise. File clerks were a dime a dozen, and they could do without me. My job would be to make sure that if the FBI found anything interesting OSS would know about it. It was clear to me that Egbert and Poole didn't attach much importance to this matter. Still, it would get me out of the files for a while longer!

'Of course,' I said.

Poole slid off the edge of the desk. 'The FBI agent you'll be working with is outside, let me introduce you.'

Poole opened the door, and a man in his late thirties entered the room. He was dressed conservatively, in suit and tie, like all G-men, but his grey fedora sported a small yellow feather stuck in the hatband.

'Mrs Pearlie,' Poole said, 'this is Special Agent Gray Williams.'

I knew his name. We had met before.

'Mrs Pearlie,' Williams said, 'it's nice to meet you.'

The man didn't remember me! Thank God!

His handshake was firm and dry. I hoped mine wasn't damp!

'Special Agent Williams,' I responded. 'Good morning.'

Special Agent Williams was the FBI agent who'd paid a terrifying call on me at my OSS office last summer. He'd gotten a report from a guest at the Wardham Hotel that I had been behaving in a 'loose fashion' with a foreigner, a Frenchman, in the bar. And that I'd made a 'spectacle of myself' at the Shoreham the following Saturday evening. The FBI had investigated me! Williams had then informed me that since I appeared to have an exemplary record, he wanted to warn me that it wasn't acceptable for a government girl with Top Secret clearance to socialize with foreign nationals.

The Frenchman was Lionel Barbier, cultural attaché at the French embassy, and, dear God, if the FBI had discovered what we'd actually accomplished that Saturday night I might be whiling away long cold and lonely hours at the Women's Federal Prison in West Virginia right now!

Of course, I'd apologized for my behavior, blaming my inexperience with champagne, and promised to be more circumspect when choosing my friends.

And now I had my very own FBI file, along with thousands of other Americans.

What were the odds that I would ever see Agent Williams again, much less be assigned to work with him? I couldn't work with him, I just couldn't! What if he remembered me? If he did he'd watch my behavior, professional and otherwise, like a hawk.

Of course, my appearance had changed since then. I wore my hair pinned up at work. I'd exchanged my harlequin eyeglass frames for new rimless round ones. And I'd lost weight. Not intentionally, but the shortage of sugar had forced me to cut down on Coca Cola, Hershey's chocolate bars, and dessert. And I suppose that the few minutes we'd spent together in an empty conference room at OSS were not seared into his memory the way they were in mine!

Domestic intelligence was the FBI's job, and they did it very well. Although our assignment would be to investigate the Martins, and the postcard I now wished I'd never set eyes on, he'd be working with me daily and might still remember me.

And then there was Joe. He was a 'foreigner'. What if Williams found out about us?

I needed to think of a way to refuse this assignment.

Mentally, I reviewed excuses. I was just a woman, a research assistant. I wasn't trained for this. Blood made me faint. I had a heart murmur. I racked my brain for a way out.

'Mrs Pearlie,' Williams said, 'I saw the commendation in your file. It seems you're wasted in the Registry! I look forward to working with you.'

Wasted in the Registry! Yes, I was indeed. And this assignment would get me away from the files, even if only for a couple of days. The more work I could do that distinguished me from most file clerks, the more likely it was

I might get another promotion and keep working after the war. How would Williams find out about Joe and me? Discretion was my middle name.

'Thank you, Agent Williams,' I said. 'I look forward to working with you, too.'

FIVE

'I don't know,' Joan said. 'I'm not sure it's such a good idea.'
We edged our way through the crowd in the OSS cafeteria toward the only two seats we could see before someone else got there. I had to lift my tray over the head of an Air Force officer wearing an OSS patch and an arm sling, and Joan, who was a large woman, used her hips to clear a path. It was a miracle that we found two seats together.

Of course, we shouldn't have discussed my new assignment, but I trusted Joan like a sister, and we were within the OSS campus. And the noise level in the room added another layer of protection. We had to lean close together to be heard.

'Why not?' I said. 'I am so frustrated working in those damn files every single day. Who knows when I might get another chance to work in the field.'

'I know,' Joan said, 'but you understand the FBI looks at every single foreigner as a potential enemy. What does this man friend of yours do, anyway?'

I had told Joan very little about Joe, and I couldn't blow his cover. 'He's teaching Slavic languages at Georgetown University,' I said.

'Good God,' Joan said, tucking into her jellied ham loaf, 'he could be a Bolshevik!'

I knew she was teasing, but I still defended Joe. 'He is not. Actually, he's lived in England most of his life. He went to university there, then taught at London University.'

'Even better. British universities are hotbeds of Socialism.'

'Stop it,' I said, pushing macaroni and cheese around my plate. I wished I had selected the tuna casserole. Joan seemed to be able to eat anything, no matter how unappetizing, but if I wasn't careful I'd lose so much weight that I'd need new clothes, and I couldn't afford them! I spread the despised oleo over a hot roll, generously, to add calories.

'Dearie,' Joan said, 'that is how the FBI thinks, you know that. If this FBI agent partner of yours learns you're more than boarding in the same house with this man you could be fired. Or at least lose your security clearance!'

If only Joan knew this particular FBI agent was the same man who'd warned me off spending time with a foreign national just a year ago!

I couldn't turn down this assignment. Williams wouldn't find out about Joe. I'd just keep my head down for the few days it would take to clear up the postcard issue.

Betty, a ninety-words-per-minute typist, eased into the chair that opened up next to us. I hadn't seen her much since the OSS reorganization, she was stuck in a typing pool somewhere now, so I gave her a quick hug around the neck. She'd changed so much in the last few months! Once so khaki-wacky she'd gotten into serious trouble, she now seemed almost staid. She'd stopped rinsing her hair platinum and it had returned to its natural ash blonde shade. She'd moderated the color of her lipstick and nail polish too, from fire engine red to a softer pink. All because of a DC Metropolitan policeman in his forties named Ralph.

She fluttered her left hand toward us, and we admired her engagement ring, a modest silver circle set with a blue stone.

'How nice!' I said. 'When is the wedding?'

'In the spring,' she said, 'when the cherry blossoms are blooming. Won't it be pretty? My parents are coming, and Ralph's brother and his family.'

'I am so excited for you,' Joan said. She was envious, too. Despite her wealth and a posse of friends, Joan didn't have a beau. She was thirty-two years old and face-to-face with spinsterhood. Over six feet tall with a booming jolly laugh, she just didn't seem to attract men interested in romance. It was their loss in my opinion.

Betty poked her fork around the food on her plate. 'I don't think this was a good choice,' she said about the macaroni and cheese. 'I am sick of cheese. Who said it was a good substitute for beef? I would so love a steak again.' She set her fork down. 'At least I'll look wonderful in my wedding dress. I've set two aside at Woody's. When the weather clears, Joan, would you come help me decide? And help me pick out my trousseau? I can't afford much, and it will have to last me the rest of the war. You have such lovely clothes.'

'I'd be happy to,' Joan said. She'd be a sport and go, even if her teeth were clenched with envy.

Betty started and grabbed my arm. 'Oh my God!' she said, softly.

'What is it?' I asked.

'John Wayne!'

'Where?' Joan asked. 'Are you sure?'

Betty nodded at a table behind us, and Joan and I swiveled in our chairs.

The actor sat with John Ford, the famous director who headed OSS's Field Photographic Unit. Ford had directed Wayne in *Stagecoach*. Wayne was so handsome, I couldn't take my eyes off him. Female heads swiveled all around him, but he and Ford seemed oblivious, deep in conversation.

'God, he is luscious!' Joan said.

'He's tall enough even for you,' Betty said. 'He must be six foot four!'

'Six-six, I'll bet,' Joan said.

'Joan, you could get General Donovan to introduce you!'

'He's married,' Joan said.

'Not any more,' Betty said. 'He's separated from his wife. I read it in *Photoplay*. He does have four children, but you could hire a nanny when they visit.'

'You're being ridiculous!'

'Is he joining Ford's unit? He must be,' I said. 'Why else would he be here?'

'Imagine having John Wayne wandering the halls,' Betty said. 'I wouldn't have any trouble getting to work in the morning, no matter how cold it was.'

'He'd be in the field most of the time,' I said.

'Hush,' Joan said, rolling her eyes. 'I happen to know he won't be joining us.'

'Tell all,' I said. 'Why not?'

Joan leaned in and whispered to us. We could just barely hear her over the noise of the crowded cafeteria.

'There aren't any officer slots left in Ford's unit. And the government doesn't want Wayne enlisting as a private. They don't think that pictures of him peeling potatoes, or God forbid bleeding on a stretcher somewhere, would be good for the country's morale.'

'So what is he going to do?' I asked.

'Stay on the USO circuit,' Joan answered.

'The press will be all over him,' I said.

Joan shrugged.

Two strapping Army officers appeared behind us, glaring. They needed our seats, and we'd been ogling the Duke long enough.

'Time to go,' Joan said. But I caught her taking one last long look at the man who was tall enough for her.

'So,' Joe said, 'what do you think?'

'I love it,' I said. And I did. The houseboats I remembered from the Cape Fear River were more like floating wooden shanties. This one was a modern motorboat. Powered by an Evinrude engine, the driver could stand on the deck and steer it with a wheel mounted on the cabin. If he had any gas, of course! The name *Miriam* was painted in silver on the hull.

The *Miriam* had a metal hull painted bright white trimmed in aqua, round portholes and a front porch that would seat four, with a rooftop sun deck reachable by a ladder, though it was hard to believe that it would ever be warm enough to sunbathe again.

The chill wind off the Potomac rattled the rigging of the sailboat moored nearby. Ice coated the piers and handrails of the dock and froze boats in their moorings. The bright sun seemed to give off no heat at all, just reflecting off the water and ice so brilliantly that I had to shade my eyes.

'It's got a good heater,' Joe said, anxious to please me. 'Let's go inside.'

The houseboat's metal sheathing blocked the wind, so inside the temperature was bearable.

'See,' Joe said, gesturing toward a miniature pot-bellied stove with one burner. 'You stoke the stove with coal and wood – Lev said it takes just a few minutes to get toasty – and you can make coffee or scramble eggs on the burner.'

I imagined the inside of the houseboat when it was cozy and warm. There was a dinette, a settee that opened into a double bed, a lavatory, an icebox, a couple of storage cabinets, and even a shower. The fabric on the curtains and upholstery was a gay red and white check splashed with blue anchors. The wood cabinets and drawers gleamed.

'So what do you think?' Joe asked again.

'I love it!' I said.

'So you'll come?' he asked, his voice breaking just a bit.

'Of course,' I said, and my voice showed my emotions too, squeaking a little.

'Maybe next weekend,' Joe said, taking both my hands. 'At the latest, the weekend after that.'

My stomach clenched, whether from nerves or anticipation I couldn't really tell. We locked eyes, our cold breath fogging around us, while Joe's grip on my hands tightened.

'I can't believe it,' I said.

'Truthfully,' Joe said, 'I'll believe it when we are actually here together. Otherwise I don't think I could get through the next week in one piece.'

Just Joe and me alone together. For two entire days. No Phoebe. No Ada. No Henry. No Dellaphine or Madeleine. I was fond of them all – well, all except Henry – but I didn't want them to know about our love affair, and neither did Joe. Love affair! Was I really going to go ahead with this?

Joe pulled me into his arms. I felt his soft beard on my cheek, then his mouth on mine, and then his tongue, and suddenly I was warmer than I had been in a very long time.

Joe was the first to pull away. 'We can't,' he said. 'Lev could be back at any moment.'

'I know,' I said.

'He said there's a good café across the street,' Joe said. 'That's where he eats most of his meals. Let's go get some coffee.'

The wharf where the *Miriam* was docked jutted out from

Maine Street, which ran along the shore of the Washington Channel of the Potomac River. It was roughly halfway between the Washington Yacht Club and the steamship berths of the Potomac River Line. Maine Street dead-ended a couple of miles west, at the Army War College near the mouth of the Anacostia River, which in turn sheltered the Navy Shipyard.

So *Miriam* was quite secure. And so were her many neighbors. Every berth on every dock on the Potomac was taken. The housing situation in Washington was so critical that people lived on houseboats, converted tugs, sailboats, basically anything with a cabin that floated, and even some quite grand yachts.

In the summer, laundry floated from rigging and people relaxed on deck chairs drinking beer with records playing in the background. Dock-mates cooked hamburgers on barbeques on the dock on the weekends. Bathing beauties decorated the sun decks.

But in this weather the boat decks and the docks were deserted. Icicles hung from sailboats' rigging, and the motorboats were imprisoned in the ice. I saw few people. They must either be inside their cabins or out looking for someplace warm, like a library or movie theatre, to spend part of the day.

Dinghies, used to get from a deep anchorage to the shore, floated behind the big sailboats too clumsy to dock. Frank Knox, the Secretary of the Navy, lived on the Presidential yacht, the *Sequoia*, which was berthed at the Yacht Club. The Potomac itself was thick with navy warships and transport vessels. Patrol boats cruised the river, concentrating at the mouth of the river during the day when the submarine-net gates were open.

Clutching our hats to our heads and bent into the wind, Joe and I hurried down the dock towards shore, but were stopped by a coast guardsman with a war dog on a leash. The guardsman was wrapped up in a heavy pea coat, scarf, and foul-weather trousers and boots. The dog wore a warm wool coat too, navy blue with the USG insignia. Laced-up canvas booties protected his feet. Other than that he didn't look much like a war dog. He was a poodle!

'Ma'am,' the seaman said, touching his cap. 'I'm Petty Officer Silva, Coast Guard port security.'

'Is something wrong?' Joe asked.

Instantly, the petty officer was on the alert, casually slipping his submarine gun from his shoulder to his free arm. 'You're not an American, sir? Russian?'

Joe spoke excellent English, but he trilled his 'r's softly, and occasionally substituted a 't' for a 'th.'

'No, Czech,' Joe said, reaching into his coat pocket for his papers before being asked. 'I have a British passport and an American visa.'

Petty Officer Silva leafed through Joe's passport. 'How do you come to have a British passport, sir?'

'I lived in London for years, teaching Slavic Languages at London University. When the war began I was recruited to teach here for the duration,' he said.

'Very good,' Silva said, handing Joe's papers back to him. 'And you, ma'am?' he said, nodding in my direction.

'I'm a file clerk. I work for the government.'

'Enjoying a nice walk on this freezing cold morning?'

'We were looking at a friend's houseboat,' Joe said.

The petty officer slung his submachine gun back over his shoulder. He gave a sign and his dog stood, wagging his tail. It must have been the canine sign for 'at ease'.

The dog was jet black, his thick wiry hair cut evenly over his muscled body.

'Can I pet him?' I asked.

'Sure, now you can.'

I scratched the dog behind the ears, and he licked my hand. 'I've never seen a poodle war dog before,' I said.

'Poodles are smart,' the petty officer said, 'and strong. They're real dogs. It's too bad civilian owners give them those sissy haircuts.'

Joe opened the café door for me, and we found a seat at a table. The elderly Negro waiter came and took our order for coffee. 'We got plenty left since it's Saturday,' he said. 'Sugar, too.' When he returned with our cups the coffee was dark and hot. Feeling started to return to my hands.

'I hate it when you're questioned because of your accent,' I said.

Joe shrugged. 'Can't be helped. People are frightened and suspicious. It could be worse. Imagine if I was Italian, or French, or even German.'

I lowered my voice. 'What if someone decides to check out your job?'

Joe shrugged that off too. 'The JDC has the connections to protect me. Don't worry, I'll be fine.' Joe drained his coffee. 'I have to go to the office today,' he said, reaching for my hand. 'Let me take you home first.'

'Not necessary,' I said. 'I have to work today too.'

As instructed by Agent Williams, I stood outside the Washington Public Library, one of Andrew Carnegie's stunning contributions to his country, huddled up against the leeward side of the great stone staircase, as if waiting for a friend to pick me up.

At the exact prearranged time an old square-bodied Ford Woody station wagon with regular DC license plates pulled up to the library. Williams was driving, his fedora, with its silly yellow feather stuck in the ribbon, pulled low over his face. I hurried down the steps. Williams leaned across the front seat and opened the door. I slid inside.

Williams shifted gears. 'I figure,' he said, 'that we should get to the Martins after Leroy goes to work. That way we, or rather you, can question Anne again. You don't need a cover. I'm just your driver, by the way.'

'We should avoid St Leonard,' I said. 'I might be recognized, and then everyone in the town would know the Martins were getting a second visit from the government.'

'Agreed,' Williams said. 'We'll stop for gas and to use the rest room in Prince Frederick. Is there a way to get to the Martins' house without going through St Leonard?'

'Not really,' I said. 'Not without a boat! But I don't think we'll attract any attention. The road through St Leonard leads to the Solomons Island training base, so plenty of unfamiliar cars pass through the town.'

'You know,' Williams said as he shifted gears and moved

out into traffic, 'I believe we've met. You look familiar. Your name is too, and Pearlie is uncommon.'

My heart began to race. 'Perhaps,' I said. 'Maybe someone introduced us at a bar, or at restaurant? I don't remember you, but I've met so many new people since moving to Washington.'

'Maybe,' he said, losing interest in the conversation as he navigated the still icy roads of Massachusetts Avenue.

Sure enough we motored through St Leonard uneventfully, turning down the rough track that led to the Martins' home.

'If you see Leroy's truck,' Williams said, 'duck down and I'll back out as if I took a wrong turn.'

The truck was gone. Williams abandoned the FBI dress code long enough to exchange his fedora for a wool cap.

Anne Martin opened the door to my knock. 'My husband's not here,' she said.

'That's okay,' I said, 'but I came to speak to you. This is Mr Williams, my driver, do you mind if he comes inside with me? It's awfully cold.'

'I have no idea what else you might need from me, but of course you can come in, both of you,' Anne Martin said.

Williams doffed his cap and said, 'Thank you, Ma'am.'

Anne led us to the sitting room but didn't offer us any refreshments. I sat on the couch with her, and Agent Williams took a chair at the table and removed a pulp novel from his coat pocket to read. The man was a good actor. Still, I wasn't sure that a cap and a dime Western transformed him from an FBI agent into a bored workingman. Anne kept glancing at him.

'I don't understand why you've come back,' Anne said. 'Didn't we answer all your questions the last time you were here?'

'Just following up,' I said. 'The postcard originated in a, shall we say, sensitive part of France.'

'I'm not comfortable talking about any of this without my husband,' she said, crossing her arms.

'Well, then, perhaps we could arrange to return sometime when both of you are here.'

'No!' she answered, more strongly than necessary, but then

subsided. 'My husband wouldn't like that. Go ahead and ask your questions. Let's get it over with.'

I wondered if Anne's husband treated her badly. I saw no physical evidence of manhandling. Her manner was relaxed and direct, and she seemed cheerful enough. Perhaps she just wanted to avoid Leroy's chronic unpleasantness.

Williams crossed his legs at the ankle and turned a page of his novel.

'You're from South Africa originally, is that correct?'

'Yes. I came to the United States with my grandmother. After the Boer War.'

'What about your parents?'

'They died. And we lost all our property during the war.'

'I'm so sorry.'

Anne shrugged. 'It was a long time ago. I've put it behind me.'

'You and your husband met this Richard Martin only once?' I asked.

'Yes,' she said. 'Before the war. His ship was docked in the Potomac, and he had time off, he said. He came to visit Leroy. Leroy had no idea who he was until Richard drew him a family tree.'

'Didn't you think that was odd?'

'Of course. But he seemed eager to make contact with us. He said he had few relatives.'

'And he talked about his mother?'

'He said he had a mother living. That's all I remember.'

'Do you have any idea why he sent you a postcard from France? It's expensive.'

'None at all. Why would I? And I don't care, either! My husband and I aren't responsible for some distant relative who sent us a silly postcard!'

'Just one more question, I promise,' I said. 'Why do you think he mentioned the date of your birthday?'

'I have no idea! He visited us the day after my birthday, his only visit! We served him leftover cake. And no, I don't remember what kind of cake! Don't you people have anything else to do than ask me all these questions, over and over again?'

'Mrs Martin—' I said.

'I want you to go now,' she said. 'I need to go to work. I open our little library several afternoons a week. And please don't bother us again!'

'Of course,' I said. 'Williams, time to leave.'

Williams stuck his paperback in his pocket and followed me to the door, where we bundled up in our heavy coats. Anne removed her apron and stood with her arms crossed, waiting for us to leave.

'Thank you—' I began.

'You're welcome,' she interrupted, opening the door for us.

Williams touched his cap and we left the house.

Once in the car, as we crunched down the track towards the road, Williams asked what I thought of the conversation.

'She makes sense,' I said, 'but . . .'

'But what?'

'I sensed that she was defiant, not just irritated. And she was not at all frightened.'

Williams nodded. 'I agree. I think this matter requires a little more thought.'

Just before we reached the bridge that crossed the little creek, Williams turned off the road to the right, bumping over a sand and crushed oyster shell path into the shelter of the woods that ran down to the inlet. He parked the car in a small clearing across the road from the cottage and near the head of the inlet.

'What are you doing?' I asked.

'Getting out of sight until Anne leaves.'

A few minutes later we saw Anne peddle by on a bicycle, so bundled up that she looked like a bear riding a tricycle at the circus.

'Let's go,' Williams said.

'Where?'

'We're going to search the house.'

Williams opened the rear door of the Woody and retrieved two torches and a Colt revolver. He handed me a torch, put one in his pocket, and shoved the Colt into a shoulder holster I hadn't noticed before.

'If you need to use the torch, shield it as much as possible,' he said to me.

We hiked down the track to the Martins' house. Anne had left a light on in the kitchen. I looked back in the direction of the Woody, but couldn't see it. The thick, low branches of the cypress trees hid it completely.

'Here's hoping she left the door open,' Williams said.

He turned the knob, and the door quietly opened into the foyer. He quickly closed it.

'I'd like it if you searched the bedrooms and bathroom,' he said. 'I think a woman would be more likely to notice anything unusual there. I'll take the sitting room and the desk.'

I kept my gloves on and mentally reviewed the search techniques I'd learned at the Farm.

The cottage had only one bedroom, occupied by a double brass bed with a side table and a double dresser. I opened every drawer, patting down the contents and sliding my hands between the folds of underwear, sweaters and nightwear.

Pulling out the drawers I felt every surface for documents that might have been taped there.

The top of the dresser appeared to be Leroy's territory. It held a man's brush and comb, an ashtray with a few coins, a ring with several keys and a cheap ballpoint pen.

The side table next to the bed was Anne's. It contained a library book, Mary Roberts Rinehart's *The Wall*. I shuffled the book's pages, looking for notes, before placing it back exactly where it had lain. The other objects on the side table surprised me. One was a lovely crystal carafe with a water glass perched on top of it. I pulled off a glove and tapped it with a finger. It rang out – quality lead crystal. The brush, comb and mirror set were silver, polished until they gleamed.

Next I opened the small drawer in the little table. A leather jewelry case rested on a photograph in a silver frame. I opened the case, and the contents took my breath away. These were real too, I was sure. A lovely strand of fat pearls with a diamond clasp rested on black velvet. Why would Anne own such things? I wondered if her family in South Africa had been wealthy. It made sense that Anne's grandmother would have brought only portable valuables from South Africa when they emigrated. I couldn't imagine that Anne had the opportunity to wear them during her current hardscrabble life.

The faded black and white photograph showed a large whitewashed farmhouse porch in an alien landscape. I had no idea what Africa looked like, but this scene conjured Africa in my imagination. Five people sat on the farmhouse porch in a wicker furniture set, wearing their best clothes for the family portrait. They were clearly a husband, wife and three children: a teenaged boy, a young girl, and an even younger boy. They appeared to be prosperous. The man had a heavy chain hanging from his watch pocket. The woman was wearing a pearl necklace, though I couldn't tell if it was the one in Anne's drawer. Ruffles cascaded down the girl's dress. A lace collar covered her neck and shoulders.

I turned the photograph frame over and read the five names written in ink on the back. *Mama, Pappa, Peter, Christiaan, Anne*. This had to be Anne's family. It must have been taken before the war and before her parents died. I wondered about the boys and what had happened to them. For all I know they'd stayed in South Africa. Anne had told me she barely remembered those times, but this photograph and the pearls were mementos. I felt guilty for disturbing her memories. Anne's unhappy past could have nothing to do with a postcard from her husband's French cousin.

I slid under the bed, flicked on my torch and examined the underside of the mattress. Nothing. The closet contained both men's and women's clothing, all ironed to perfection. A shotgun and a Remington rifle leaned up against the back of the closet.

I finished my search with the tiny bathroom; it was spotless and smelled of bleach. A big cast-iron bathtub, a small sink and a toilet furnished it, with barely enough room for a standard sized human to move around. The medicine cabinet contained toothbrushes, toothpaste, aspirin, witch hazel, an unopened package of Ivory soap and a jar of Vicks VapoRub.

I found Williams in the sitting room, carefully replacing

papers in a roll top desk. 'There is nothing interesting here,' he said, 'except what you'd expect. Pay stubs and a ledger. Leroy is an oysterman, but he works for the cannery when he can't dredge. I've been through an envelope of receipts, his checkbook, and a calendar. That's it. Find anything?'

'Anne's past,' I said.

'Tell me later,' he said, glancing at his watch. 'We need to finish. Anne could get home any time. I'd like to get a look in the storage shed, but I can see a big padlock on the door from here.'

'There are some keys on Leroy's dresser,' I said.

'Get them,' he said.

I retrieved Leroy's keys, memorizing the position of the ring, and met Williams outside. He unlocked the heavy padlock.

'Put the keys back,' he said. 'That way if we hear Anne's bicycle we can quickly latch the padlock and take off through the woods.'

Back in the house I carefully replaced the keys, and then instinct suggested I search the kitchen. The stollen Anne had made the first time I came here, the sugar in the bowl for our tea, made me wonder. Sure enough in the icebox I found meat – a roast and two steaks – and plenty of butter. There was a two-pound bag of sugar in the cupboard.

Of course, in the country it was easier to avoid rationing.

Back out in the cold I found Williams in the shed.

'Take a look at this!' he said, lifting two gas jerry cans up for me to see. I could hear liquid sloshing inside.

'And over there,' he said, nodding towards a corner. Two tires, with at least half their tread remaining, leaned up against the clapboard wall.

'Hoarding,' I said. 'Their refrigerator is full of meat and butter.'

'I could confiscate this now,' Williams said. He set the cans down, careful to line them up with their outlines in the dust. 'But I don't think I will. I don't want to get Leroy's wind up, at least not until we're sure the postcard business is harmless.'

I glanced around the rest of the storage shed. It was full of

the usual tools of an oysterman, at least as far as I knew –
baskets and ropes, chains and buckets. A crab cooker sat in a
corner.

'Let's go,' Williams said, dusting off his hands. 'We don't
want Anne to find us here.'

We reached the shelter of the trees seconds before Anne
came down the driveway on her bicycle.

Williams dropped me off on a corner two blocks from my
boarding house. It was late; Williams and I had stopped for a
fried chicken dinner on the way home. I walked cautiously
over icy streets through an iron grey dusk, so cold I could
hardly feel my feet, grabbing at streetlights and mailboxes to
keep from slipping and falling.

It was strange that I thought of 'Two Trees' as my home
now. I felt sort of guilty about it. Wasn't home the sun-faded
white clapboard house in Wilmington I'd lived in for most
of my life? Or the tiny apartment over the Wilmington
Western Union office I'd shared with my husband before he
died?

My life in Washington, at OSS, at 'Two Trees', over the
past year, felt more real to me than all the years that had
gone before. The world was in the midst of a great and
terrible war. Civilization itself was endangered. Friends
and relatives were dying far from home. Great nations had
already been conquered. It all reminded me of Revelation,
which my pastor at home preached to us constantly, about
the final battle of good and evil. I was a part of it all in my
own small way. Maybe that was why I felt everything more
intensely than I ever had before. From eating a good meal
to dreaming about lovemaking with Joe, life took on a new
intensity. I was alive, when so many had died, and I felt it
every day.

'I was raised on this,' Dellaphine said, 'but I never thought
I'd be serving it for Sunday dinner in Miss Phoebe's dining
room. I about fell out when I saw the recipe in that Betty
Crocker booklet the ration people give out.'

'Gave out, Momma,' Madeleine said. Madeleine was

Dellaphine's twenty-year-old daughter who worked as a typist at the Social Security Administration, punching out Social Security cards on a special typewriter. She was a graduate of Washington's best colored high school, and she couldn't help but correct her mother's grammar.

'Hush,' Dellaphine said. 'I'm too old to change the way I talk. You understood me, didn't you?'

Madeleine shrugged and went on turning the pages of the Sunday edition of *The Afro-American*. Thanks to the big cooking range, the kitchen was the warmest room in the house, which was why Madeleine and I were both sitting at the kitchen table watching Dellaphine make scrapple for our Sunday dinner. Phoebe insisted on the old Southern tradition of a big meal after church, though she and Dellaphine were the only people in the household who went to church much. Dellaphine went to an early service so she could get back to cook. She still wore her church outfit, a black and red checked dress with a wide belt that made her look even skinnier than she was.

Dellaphine had already simmered a pound of fresh pork in salt water until it was tender. After it cooled she shredded it finely, then put it back in the pot of pork stock. When it began to bubble she slowly added cornmeal to it, stirring it constantly. After the mixture thickened she seasoned it with pepper and sage. Then she poured the mixture into a greased baking dish and put it in the icebox to set. Right before dinner she'd cut the mixture into half-inch slices and brown them in bacon fat. She'd already mashed potatoes and added margarine to a pot of green beans. The dishes rested on the hob. When she put the scrapple in the icebox I saw a cherry Jell-O mold spotted with fruit cocktail, our dessert. When I'd first come to 'Two Trees' dessert was always pie or cake, but no more.

Scrapple and Jell-O, Henry would not be happy!

We boarders were fortunate to get the meals we did – breakfast during the week, dinner Monday through Thursday, and Sunday lunch. Most boarding houses in Washington didn't offer any meals at all. Much of the DC workforce had to fend for themselves in the crowded cafes and cafeterias of the city. Boarders were packed three to a room, sometimes even sleeping in shifts, three people living out of one dresser and one closet! A dozen people might share one bathroom.

Henry, Joe, Ada and I knew how lucky we were, so we helped out as much as we could. Ada and I made our own beds with sheets fresh from Dellaphine's iron and helped in the kitchen. In the summer I'd tended a Victory Garden and a flock of chickens. Henry and Joe chopped wood for the sitting room fire and took care of Phoebe's car.

Ada and I each had our own room on the second floor down the hall from Phoebe's. The three of us shared a big bathroom with two sinks. We lived in fear that someone from the Washington Housing Authority would show up to inspect the house and insist that Phoebe take in two more girls!

'Baby,' Dellaphine said to Madeleine, 'you set the table yet?'

'I'll do it now,' Madeleine said, shrugging.

'You should 'a done it already.'

I waited for Madeleine to explode, but for once she bit her lip. She did chores grudgingly, as if to put distance between herself and the domestic job she might have had to settle for before the war. Like me, she was saving for college or her own apartment.

'I've done the table already,' Ada said, coming into the kitchen, dressed in turquoise silk, her platinum hair tucked into a matching snood and her new mink thrown over her shoulder.

'Where are you going?' I asked.

'I'm playing at a tea dance this afternoon,' Ada said, sitting down at the table with us, the mink thrown over the back of a kitchen chair. Madeleine reached over and stroked the thick fur softly.

'The Willard's power must be back on,' I said.

'It is, and it's not going to be as cold tonight, the radio says. The hotel's sending a cab for me. I'll leave right after dinner.'

'As soon as Miss Phoebe gets home we'll fry up the scrapple and eat,' Dellaphine said.

*　　*　　*

I was carrying dirty dishes into the kitchen when the telephone rang. I heard Henry pick up the receiver.

'Louise! It's for you!' he called.

Madeleine took the plates from me, and I wiped my hands on a dishtowel as I went into the hall, where our only telephone sat on a table near the foot of the staircase. The telephone was ancient, but a repairman down the street kept reviving it. Which was good, since to buy a new telephone Phoebe would need to file an application with the government.

'Hello,' I said into the speaker. Williams spoke to me from the other end of the line. The one-way conversation went on for several minutes. 'Of course,' I answered him.

I poked my head into the sitting room, where Henry, Joe and Phoebe had gathered around the fire for coffee. Ada had already left.

'I'd like to know how she got that mink,' Henry said, referring to Ada. 'She couldn't afford it herself, could she?'

Phoebe ignored him, shuffling through the *Washington Post* for the funny papers.

'One of her boyfriends gave it to her, probably,' Henry said. 'Phoebe, you should talk to her; her behavior reflects on you, you know.'

'Ada's personal life is none of our concern,' Joe said, in a tone of voice that sent Henry back to the editorials, muttering. Phoebe didn't raise her eyes from the cartoons.

I tapped gently on the doorframe to get their attention. 'I'm going to have to spend the rest of the day and the night out,' I said. 'Maybe two nights. That was the house doctor from the Mayflower Hotel. My friend Joan is ill, and they need someone to stay the night with her.'

'Is it serious?' Phoebe asked, passing a cup of steaming coffee to Joe.

'The doctor thinks she'll be fine, it's just a little fever, but he wants to make sure she's not alone.'

'Do you want me to drive you there?' Joe asked. 'It's still so cold.'

'No, it's not necessary, it's not far. I can catch a taxi or walk if I need to. I'm going upstairs to change and pack an overnight bag before I leave.'

I waited on the corner of 'K' and '21st', just four blocks from the Mayflower Hotel, but that wasn't where I was headed. I made a mental note to call Joan as soon as possible so she'd be ready to verify my alibi if necessary.

'We'll freeze,' were the first words I said to Agent Williams after he picked me up, this time in a different car, a maroon Ford Coupe with Maryland plates.

'No, we won't,' he said, tossing my overnight bag into the back seat next to a pile of khaki clothing. 'I've brought cold weather gear for both of us. The Army designed it for the Aleutians, so we'll be warm enough. And I've got a thermos of coffee and some sandwiches. Ever been on a stakeout before?'

'No,' I said, trying to sound calm and self-confident. 'But, of course, we learned stakeout strategy at the Farm.'

A stakeout! How thrilling! I would have to be more than just a little cold to miss that experience. I told myself I was padding my personnel file, so as to seem more valuable to OSS, but really I was just plain excited.

Williams pulled out into sparse afternoon traffic and headed east toward the Maryland shore.

'I've reserved two rooms at a guesthouse in St Leonard for a couple of days. Tell me, when you were here with Collins, in the café, did you mention being with any specific government agency?'

'Yes, the Office of Price Administration.'

'Good. That works. Our cover is, I've replaced Collins. You're my assistant. That should give us plenty of excuse for snooping.'

'But what about the Martins? Will they buy that? Collins and I both questioned them about the postcard.'

'I know,' Williams said. 'We aren't planning to make contact with the Martins, just watch them for a couple of days. I doubt they mentioned the postcard to anyone else. You know how people around here feel about foreigners. Leroy and Anne wouldn't want their neighbors to know they're getting mysterious postcards from occupied France.'

The day was fading into dusk when we pulled into a guesthouse parking lot just off St Leonard Road. It was a rambling, shingled old farmhouse with a barn out back. A middle-aged woman with hair the color of fog answered the doorbell. She wore a man's rubber boots, over heavy trousers, and a thick cable knit sweater. Her cheeks were bright red from the cold. An English springer spaniel followed on her heels, ears flopping with each step.

'I was outside in the shed feeding the milk cow,' she said. 'It's lucky I heard the doorbell.'

'We have reservations for two rooms for two nights,' Williams said. 'I'm Mr Williams, and this is my assistant, Mrs Pearlie. We're from the Office of Price Administration.'

'I'm Lenore Sullivan,' she said. 'Welcome to St Leonard.'

Mrs Sullivan sat down at a desk in the hall and drew a ledger from a stack of papers. The dog lay at her feet, her eyes fixed on us, protecting her mistress.

'Here,' she said, opening the ledger, 'sign here. You've got rooms one-oh-one and one-oh-two, just upstairs. You're the only guests. And I don't do meals in the winter, just the summer season. I'm sorry, the only place you can get dinner tonight would be at the fountain at the Esso station. But tomorrow Bertie's Café will be open all day.' She handed us our keys.

'Thank you,' Williams said. 'But we didn't expect to find a place open on Sunday. We brought sandwiches. And we'll be working late tonight.'

Mrs Sullivan looked at us quizzically, wondering, I expected, what on earth a couple of Washington bureaucrats would be working on at night in the tiny town of St Leonard, but Williams didn't offer any explanation. The fewer lies we told the better.

Half an hour later we were back in the car headed to our stakeout. For once Williams had abandoned his FBI agent uniform of suit and fedora and was wearing heavy trousers, boots and a duffel coat. I'd dressed in wool trousers, my wool coat and my rubber snow boots with two pairs of socks. I still shivered with cold until the car heater warmed up.

We drove with the car headlights on low until we got to the dirt track to the Martins, then without them entirely. The moon was waxing, so we weren't completely blind, despite the ubiquitous clouds and patches of fog that floated through the trees. Williams left the track and maneuvered into the trees, parking in the tiny clearing we'd found earlier near the head of the Martins' inlet. Between thick branches I saw lights on in the Martins' cottage.

The pile of khaki clothing in the back seat of Williams' car turned out to be padded Army Mountain and Ski Parkas with fur trimmed hoods and cuffs. The one Williams handed me was large enough for me to wear over my sweater. It hung down to my knees. My torch fit neatly into one of the deep pockets. Williams fished out the thermos of coffee and sandwiches he'd brought. The coffee was lukewarm and the sandwiches were cream cheese and pickle, not my favorite, but I was hungry and thirsty enough not to care.

'What are we looking for?' I asked.

Williams didn't answer me and didn't look as though he intended to. I repressed my annoyance. Expressing it wouldn't get me anywhere.

'Listen,' I said, 'I'm sure you'd rather be doing this on your own. But I'm your liaison with the OSS, and we brought the FBI into this, whether you like it or not. Do I need to report to my superiors that you didn't keep me informed?'

Williams opened the car door and dumped the rest of his coffee on the ground. 'Okay,' he said. 'We had our agent in Baltimore telephone the local constable here. Asked him what he knew about Martin. It appears the guy can be rough, and he has some tough friends too. He's been seen driving at night where he has no business being.'

'The constable hasn't questioned him?'

Williams shrugged. 'The man is seventy-some years old. His predecessor was drafted, and he was the only guy available to take the job. Our man got the idea he's afraid of Martin.'

I was afraid of Martin too. He was big, strong and he had a temper.

'Did the sheriff say anything about his wife?' I wondered if she was afraid of Martin, too.

'Not much,' he said. 'I wondered what his hold on her was; she seems classier than him. The sheriff said they don't socialize much. She cooks meals for shut-ins and keeps the local library open part-time. He drinks at the bar with his friends a couple evenings a week, but doesn't get drunk. Oh, and he's a hunter. Bags deer every season.'

That explained the guns in his closet.

'I'm hoping that tonight, or maybe tomorrow night, he'll go out on one of his night drives so we can follow him and figure out what he might be up to. That's about all the time the Bureau is willing to give me.'

'So how do you think all this figures into the postcard the Martins got from France?'

'Not one bit, Mrs Pearlie. If you want to know my opinion, what I'm going to report to the Bureau, the postcard is just a coincidence. Whatever Martin is up to, it has nothing to do with France or Nantes or whatever.'

I didn't respond. I didn't agree with him, but I could say that when I filed my own report. If Martin was doing something illegal on his nightly forays around the western shore, it could be just a coincidence. The postcard could still be meaningful.

Heavy clouds drifted over the moon, and darkness settled all around us. Almost simultaneously the Martins' door opened, and Leroy Martin came outside so bundled up that I could hardly see his face. He strode to his truck, climbed into the cab, and started up the engine. Pulling out into the dirt track, his wheels skidded on oyster shells and he changed gears. Williams used the noise to cover the sound of cranking up our car's engine.

'There's a map in my bag in the back,' Williams said, his eyes not wavering from Martin's truck as it headed for St Leonard Road. 'Mark where we're going, don't use the torch unless it's necessary. And keep a look out – I'm going to drive without headlights if I can manage it.'

I simmered with anger – did he think I couldn't read a map? But as usual I kept my mouth shut.

Williams waited until he saw Martin turn north onto St Leonard Road, then followed him.

It wasn't easy to keep Martin's truck in sight since he drove without headlights too. As he knew the roads better than us, only the moonlight that occasionally broke through the clouds allowed us to keep up with him. I wrapped a scarf around my torch to diffuse the beam and followed Martin's progress on the map.

We headed north for several miles, then turned west on a dirt road.

'I think this is a driveway or a farm road,' I said. 'It's not marked on the map.'

Sure enough I saw Martin stop ahead at a building. We pulled into a layby sheltered by trees and cut off our engine.

'Come on,' Williams said, opening his door. 'Let's get as close as we can.'

Which wasn't close. Maybe 100 yards away from the building was a copse of loblolly pines that sheltered us from view. Williams pulled binoculars out of his jacket pocket and raised them to his eyes. 'God damn it,' he said, 'my night vision is awful. Can you see anything?' He passed the binoculars to me.

I pushed my glasses onto the top of my head and adjusted the focus. 'I see Martin,' I said. 'And there's another man with him. He must have come out of the building – it looks like a tobacco barn. The door is ajar, there's light inside.'

'What are they doing?'

'Talking. Wait, they're going into the barn together.'

'I wish we could get closer! Anything could be going on in there! Illegal gambling, moonshine—'

'Quiet,' I said. 'Here they come. They're carrying something big and heavy wrapped in canvas. It sags in the middle.'

We could hear the men's voices, cursing by their tone, as

they struggled with the unwieldy bundle. It didn't take much imagination to wonder if it was a corpse.

The moon came out, and we could see the scene more clearly. The two men carried their burden to Martin's truck, then managed to sling it into the back. Both of them got into the truck, Martin turned it around, and they headed back down the road.

'Down,' Williams whispered, and we flattened ourselves on the cold ground. We were lucky. Martin went by without noticing us or our car. When they got to the intersection with Solomons Island Road I ran out into the middle of the dirt road to see which way they turned.

'South!' I said to Williams, who was already in our car starting the engine.

We followed them south past the turnoff to Martin's house, then west.

'This is a state road,' I said. 'But it doesn't go anywhere. It dead ends at the Patuxent River. At a wharf.'

'How wide is the river?'

'About three miles across. There are two wharves and a couple of landings around here.'

'We can't lose them.'

A few minutes later, my eyes glued to the map, I felt Williams engage the brakes.

'They've stopped,' Williams said. 'Where are we?'

'Right at the river, at an inlet called Island Creek. It's a dead end.'

'Let's wait here. They've got to come back this way. Maybe they're dumping whatever they loaded into the truck into the river.'

A few minutes passed.

'Are you sure the road ends at the river?' Williams asked me.

'According to the map,' I said. 'And there aren't any side roads marked. Of course there could be tracks coming off it.'

'Let's go see,' Williams said.

Slowly, we drove down the road, until I could see the Patuxent River gleaming in the moonlight. And at the edge of the shore was a ferryboat landing that wasn't marked on the map. The truck was long gone across the river.

Williams's head dropped onto the steering wheel.

'Damn!' he said. 'Damn it! What are those guys doing! And what was their load!'

SIX

I was awakened by a rap on my door.

'Mrs Pearlie,' our hostess called.

'Yes,' I answered. 'Is it late?'

'It's only seven,' she answered, 'but I thought you might want to know that I've stoked up the boiler, and there'll be hot water if you'd like to take a bath.'

A bath! I hadn't had a real bath in a week. Mrs Sullivan must have a coal furnace.

'I'd love to, thank you!' I called out to her.

I flung off the heavy quilts I'd found piled on my bed when I got in last night and kicked out the hot water bottle tucked under the sheets.

Throwing on my bathrobe and grabbing my sponge bag, I peered into the hall outside my door. The door to Room 102, Williams' room, was closed, so I tiptoed over to the bathroom and let myself in.

It was a real bathroom, one separate from the toilet, well stocked with soap and towels. A deep claw-foot tub took up most of the space in the room.

I turned on the hot water spigot and filled the tub, steam rising from the water. I added a little cold water until I could bear the temperature, and slid down into the tub up to my neck. After soaping myself off I luxuriated as long as I thought I could get away with it, then I opened the spigot again and washed my hair.

There were towels warm from hanging over the hot water pipe. I wrapped myself in two, checked the hall, and found the coast was clear to scoot back to my room. Once inside I changed into clean underwear and a fresh blouse before putting on my 'uniform': the same tailored wool suit I'd worn yesterday.

I dried my hair as best I could, brushing it over the vent in the floor of my room. As I did I heard the bathroom pipes gurgling. Williams must be taking advantage of the hot water too.

A few minutes later I heard another knock on the door. It was Williams, of course, clean, shaven, and dressed like an FBI agent again.

'Let's get some breakfast at the café,' he said. Then he lowered his voice. 'We need to retrace our steps from last night, see if we can figure out what the hell was going on. You had the map, can you find the way?'

'Of course,' I said, annoyed that he would even ask.

We stopped at Bertie Woods' Café, where Williams and I had had lunch. We were the only customers.

The same waitress seated us and handed us menus. 'You're back,' she said to me, without warmth. She stared at Williams.

'This is my boss,' I said quickly, indicating Williams. 'We're from the Office of Price Administration.'

She stood with one hand on her hip and scrutinized us. 'Where's the fella you were with last time?' she asked me.

'Busy, I've taken his place,' Williams answered.

'Where is everyone?' I asked, trying to divert the conversation.

'Honey,' she said, 'they've come and gone. It's almost seven thirty. We get started early around here. Coffee?'

The coffee was real, not cut with a speck of chicory, and hot. The sugar was real too, and I spooned two heaping teaspoons into my mug.

We ordered eggs, bacon, and toast. When it came there were four strips of bacon on each plate, and from tasting it I could tell it was home-cured, like I was used to getting at home in North Carolina.

'People around here live pretty well,' Williams said. 'There's not a place in DC where you can get more than two strips of bacon for breakfast. They don't seem to have heard of rationing here. And that was the hottest hot water I've experienced in a very long time.' He dug into his plate greedily.

'This is the country,' I said. 'Mrs Sullivan has a coal furnace. And you can't stop people from butchering their own hogs.'

'As long as they don't sell it to someone over the controlled price, I suppose not,' Williams said.

As we left the café I heard the waitress mutter 'pencil pushers' as the door swung closed behind us.

We pulled into the Esso station, where the attendant looked at our 'A' gasoline coupon and shot us as dirty a look as I'd seen in this town so far.

'Ain't you lucky,' she said, tucking long greying hair behind an ear before she jerked the nozzle from the pump. 'Government people get all the gas they want. We got to get by on two gallons a week. So what do you two do?'

'We're from the Office of Price Administration,' Williams said.

'You can see I charge just what I'm allowed,' the attendant said, gesturing to the sign that hung over her pumps. 'Nineteen cents a gallon and not a penny more.'

The attendant ripped the nozzle out of our gas tank and took the cash and the ration coupon Williams handed her.

'You'd think the government would have better use for two able-bodied people than coming out to our little town and checking up on our prices,' she said.

As we pulled out of the filling station I saw the attendant shaking her fist at us in the rear view mirror.

'I don't think that woman would hesitate to sell Leroy a few cans of gasoline for more than the ration price, do you?' Williams asked.

'No, I do not,' I said.

'Let's see if we can find the tobacco barn,' Williams said, turning north on Solomons Island road.

About two miles out of town I spotted the unmarked dirt track that led to the barn.

'Here,' I said.

'Are you sure?'

I bit my tongue. I could read a damn map! Hadn't I proven that already? 'Positive,' I said. 'I took notes on the mileage on the odometer last night. This is it.'

We bumped over the track through pastures where cattle huddled together for warmth and bare tree limbs groped the sky. A farmhouse on a low rise overlooked the fallow tobacco fields and the herd of cattle, smoke rising from two stone chimneys. Glazed-over puddles of water collected in the low areas of the fields and on the road.

'I'm surprised those cattle are outside,' Williams said.

'The sun feels good on their backs. They'll head back to the barn when they're ready.'

The road stopped at the decrepit tobacco barn. Right behind it I could see a narrow creek – Battle Creek, according to the map – which ran into the Patuxent River. Also according to the map, a big wharf was located there. If Martin's late night run had been legitimate, wouldn't he have used the wharf in broad daylight?

There wasn't a soul around.

Williams lifted the latch that sealed the door shut, shoved on the rotted wood, and we entered the dark building. It reeked of a century's worth of tobacco and the fires that cured it. Daylight filtered through holes in the chinking, but we still had to fetch our torches to see properly.

There was nothing in the barn except for a few bales of moldering hay, a discarded rope with a rusted pulley attached, a broken wagon wheel, a kerosene lantern sitting on a hogshead, and a pile of filthy canvas on the floor.

Williams lifted a corner of the cloth. 'This is sailcloth,' he said. 'Wonder what it's doing here?'

Together we gathered up the cloth, and as it lifted from the floor, we saw a dark stain on the boards underneath.

We tossed the sailcloth aside and knelt to inspect the stain. It was blood – I recognized the odor at once. Lots of blood, soaked deeply into the wood.

I thought of the dead weight wrapped in canvas that Martin and his accomplice had carried to Martin's truck last night.

'Do you think that bundle those two men carried out of here last night could have been a corpse?'

'That possibility occurred to me, too,' he said. 'We'll know soon. The FBI can type blood in twenty-four hours now. Our crime lab is the best in the world, thanks to Director Hoover and Congress.'

He pulled a pocketknife and a small glass vial with a rubber stopper out of his pocket. He sliced a sliver of the stained wood off the rough floor and placed it carefully in the vial, stoppering it and tucking it into his suit pocket.

'I'll get it back to the lab on the next bus and put a rush on it. Look for a weapon,' Williams said. We searched the tobacco barn top to bottom and didn't find anything that could have caused a wound that would result in so much blood.

We piled the canvas back over the stain and left it looking as if no one had disturbed it, then went back outside to Martin's car.

'Let's find that ferry landing,' he said.

We drove the four or so miles back to Solomons Island Road, passing the farmhouse on the hill again, then turned almost immediately south, on Broome's Island Road, and drove the six miles to the ferry landing right on the Patuxent River.

There wasn't much to see. The road stopped at the landing, a dirt space that sloped down to the river. You wouldn't necessarily know it was a ferry landing except for the sign mounted on a leaning fencepost shoved into the sand at the edge of it.

The Patuxent was a good-sized river that ran between the Chesapeake Bay and the Potomac. During the summer it would be thick with fishing boats and skipjacks, but now it was empty except for a few chunks of floating ice and one vessel headed our way.

I grabbed Williams' arm. 'I think I see the ferryboat,' I said.

Williams lifted his binoculars to his face. 'That's it, all right.'

We watched the ferryboat, powered by a noisy engine belching black smoke, coming towards us. What remained of the ice on the river cracked and broke apart as it approached.

When the ferryboat struck the beach, a young man, a

teenager really, leapt off the boat and used its momentum to pull the boat a few extra feet up the slope, then docked it to the solitary pier.

There were two vehicles on the ferry: a truck loaded with hay bales and a car with no tread on its tires. Using the ferry saved them from driving way north to the bridge to get to the lower part of the western shore.

The truck and car motored off the ferry and on up the road, and the ferryman jumped off the deck. It was Dennis, the angry man from the café, the one who'd threatened to beat up Collins.

Dennis eyed Williams from head to foot, taking in his citified topcoat, suit and tie. 'You looking to ferry across the river?' he asked.

'No,' Williams said. 'I'm Special Agent Gray Williams, FBI. This is my assistant, Mrs Pearlie.'

Williams had abandoned our cover. I supposed it was time. We were investigating a possible serious crime.

Dennis spread his legs and put his hands on his hips, as if standing his ground. 'Son,' he said to the teenager, 'you go on board the ferry. I'll be there in just a minute.'

The boy shrugged and climbed back on board the boat.

Dennis turned back to us. 'What does a G-man want with me?' he asked.

'Why did you meet Leroy Martin's truck here in the middle of last night and take him across the river?' Williams said.

Dennis leaned his head back and laughed. 'You government people,' he said. 'You're a bunch of idiots. Any ferry can use this landing! Not just mine. There are dozens of private ferries around here. You can't prove it was me!'

'How many ferries operate in the middle of the night in this cold?' I said.

Dennis didn't even blink an eye. 'You're a fool too,' he said. 'Anyone who can drive a boat, and that's everyone who lives around here, could borrow my ferry. It's just tied up across the river.'

Williams pulled out a business card and handed it to him. 'I'm not that worn-out policeman of yours,' he said. 'I'm the FBI. You think about this. I'm going to find out what you and Leroy loaded onto that ferry last night. There was another guy, too. You'd better wise up and tell me before I arrest you.'

Dennis tore up Williams's card into tiny pieces. 'It weren't me last night,' he said. 'You keep out of my business. I got a right to protect my property, and I keep a loaded double-barreled shotgun on my boat.'

As if on cue, Dennis's son appeared on the boat with the shotgun slung over his arm.

'And I,' Williams said, opening his coat and showing Dennis his shoulder holster, 'carry a Colt .38 Super at all times.'

For just a second I saw Dennis's eyes flicker, as well they might. The Colt .38 Super could shoot through a car door.

Williams closed his coat and buttoned it, signaling the end of the confrontation. He tipped his hat to Dennis. 'I'll be seeing you,' he said. 'Don't take any vacations.'

He calmly turned, exposing his back to Dennis and his shotgun-bearing son, and we went back to our car.

I didn't like Williams, but I had to admit the man was cool. Turning his back on Dennis was an impressive display of courage, but I didn't see that he'd learned anything. We couldn't prove that Dennis was running his ferry last night, and Williams had antagonized him to boot.

Back in the car, Williams started the engine. 'Let's go talk to the farmer who lives in that house that overlooks the road,' he said. 'Maybe he saw something.'

A woman answered the door at the white farmhouse on the hill. She had a warm and welcoming expression on her face until she took in Williams. The man's suit told the people around here he was from the government. They didn't want someone from the government to knock on their door. Damn the FBI and their bloody dress code!

Williams removed his fedora. 'Good morning, ma'am,' he said. 'I'm Special Agent Gray from the FBI . . .'

Sure enough her eyes opened wide enough to touch her eyebrows and her hand gripped the doorknob. She'd been halfway to opening the door, but stopped. 'What do you want here?' she asked.

'Just making routine enquiries,' he said. 'Nothing to be concerned about.' He indicated my presence with a nod of his head. 'This is my assistant, Mrs Pearlie.'

Soon there would be nothing left of my lower lip. So, Williams had abandoned our cover, but I was apparently still his assistant!

'We need to ask you some questions,' Williams said.

'About what?'

'May we come in, please,' he said.

Reluctantly, she showed us into a warm sitting room heated by an ancient wood-fired stove. She gestured to a couch covered with a quilt. 'Have a seat. I just fixed a pot of fresh coffee, can I offer you some?'

I hurried to accept, but Williams put a hand on my arm before I got the words out.

'No, thank you, ma'am. Can I have your full name, please?' Williams asked. By the look on her face her name would be about all he would get from her.

'I'm Gladys Cooke,' she said. 'My husband Frank and I own this place.'

'And the name of it is?'

'What?' she said.

'The name of your farm,' I said. 'We just need to know for our notes.'

'I don't know why. Everyone around here knows us. This is Hilltop Farm.'

'Where is your husband today?' Williams continued.

'He works at the naval station on Solomons Island,' she said. 'Has done since it was built.'

'You can spare the time from the farm?' I asked, trying to add some friendliness to Williams' questioning.

She shrugged. 'My husband felt like it was his patriotic duty. And the money is real good. We hired a colored man to help with the chores. What is this all about?'

'Last night late a truck drove by your house, stopped at that old tobacco barn on Battle Creek Road,' Williams said, 'and loaded up a suspicious looking bundle wrapped in canvas.

Leroy Martin drove the truck, but another man was at the barn and helped Leroy load it up. Martin drove down the road to the ferry landing at Island Creek, where it caught his friend Dennis's ferry before we could reach it. Did you see or hear that truck?'

'No, sir, I did not!' she said, crossing her arms. 'We own that barn, but we ain't used it in years. It's just for storage. I didn't hear nothing last night. Why don't you talk to Dennis?'

'We did. He said someone "borrowed" his ferryboat.'

'I reckon he knows, then.'

'Inside the barn we found evidence of fresh blood, Mrs Cooke. Would you know anything about that?'

Mrs Cooke's lips compressed into a thin line. 'What makes you think you can come in here and ask me such? Like I'm a criminal! I'll thank you to get out of my house and off my property! And don't come back unless you know what you are talking about!'

Her dog, alarmed by her tone of voice, leapt to its feet and growled at us.

'Ma'am, I should warn you that the FBI—'

I couldn't stand it another minute. I stood up and reached for my coat. 'Thank you for your time, Mrs Cooke,' I said.

'Mrs Pearlie—' Williams began.

'We need to leave, now, as Mrs Cooke has requested,' I said. 'Come on!'

Outside, Williams grabbed my arm.

'Let go of me,' I said.

'What do you think you're doing?' he said.

'In the car!'

'I'm warning you . . .'

'Get in the God-damned car!' I said. 'The woman is standing on the porch watching us!'

We both got in the car, Williams slamming his door. 'Listen—' he said.

'Start the car!'

'You—!'

'Drive!'

Williams shifted gears and headed back up the road, but pulled off onto the shoulder when we were out of sight of the farmhouse. 'What was that all about?' he asked.

'What is wrong with you! You're wearing a suit, tie, and fedora. You stick out like a sore thumb around here. I grew up in Wilmington, North Carolina, a place a lot like this. You don't turn people down when they offer you a cup of coffee in their home. It's insulting!'

'Director Hoover insists we wear suits and refuse refreshments, you know that.'

'Director Hoover isn't interviewing rural working people from the western shore of Maryland! You treat people like criminals before you have any evidence!'

'What happened last night wasn't evidence?'

'You don't know what those men were doing. Once you started treating them like gangsters we sure weren't going to find out. And what was that business with the guns on the ferryboat slip? Are you crazy! You could have gotten us both shot!'

'You think you could do better?'

'I would certainly hope so.'

We drove in silence back toward St Leonard.

'I guess we should get some lunch,' he said.

'Fine. But not at Bertie Woods' Café. We've made enough of a spectacle of ourselves there.'

'There's a shack out here called Tommy's Crab House,' he said. 'That suit you, Mrs Pearlie?'

'Sure,' I said. 'But do me a favor. Ditch the hat, topcoat, and tie and wear one of the parkas so that you look like a human being.'

After lunch we drove back to Mrs Sullivan's guesthouse.

'Look,' Williams said. 'Now that I've identified myself as an FBI agent, why don't you wait here until after I've talked to the police officer? Then I'll drive you up to Frederick and you can catch a bus back to Washington.'

I'd had enough. I chose my words carefully, knowing I might damage my career if I was too strident.

'You seem to have forgotten,' I said. 'I am not your assistant.

I'm your colleague, your liaison with the Office of Strategic Services. It was our initial inquiry about a postcard from France mailed to Leroy Martin that brought us here. I am going with you to talk to the constable and everywhere else you intend to pursue this investigation. And if I feel it's necessary I'll ask my own questions.'

Williams just looked at me, not in a malevolent way, but calculating, as if he was deciding how to handle me. I held his gaze without flinching. His eyes broke away first.

'Of course,' he said. 'I apologize.'

That was all. He shifted gears, and we continued down the road toward the Post Office, where the Calvert County Constable kept an office.

The Post Office was located in Bertie Woods' Store, which was attached to the café where we had already made such an impression on the local folk. I noticed that Williams kept his parka on when we went inside. The Post Office had a separate entry, on the other side of the building from the café. Inside I noticed the building directory listed the library, where Anne worked part-time. I wondered if she was there now.

Constable Ben Long was the same man Art Collins and I had asked for directions to the Martin home what seemed like an age ago. His faded blue double-breasted police uniform had some wear on it, but the tin star pinned to his chest gleamed. A cane, marked off in inches, topped with a wicked knobbed handle, leaned against the back of his chair. His aged collie lay on a blanket nearby, but raised her head and wagged her tail, her eyes bright and alert.

Long recognized me, too. Standing up, gripping the edge of his desk for support, he stretched out a hand to shake mine.

'I'm sorry,' he said, 'but I don't remember your name.'

'I'm Mrs Louise Pearlie,' I said. 'And this is Special Agent Gray Williams.'

'FBI,' Williams said. 'You spoke on the telephone with our agent in Baltimore about Leroy Martin.'

'Of course,' Long said, shaking Williams hand too, before sitting back down in his desk chair.

Long's office was not much more than a closet behind the sorting room of the post office. It barely held Long's desk and chair, a file cabinet, and another small chair that Williams offered to me. Williams leaned up against the file cabinet. A telephone, typewriter, and banker's lamp crowded the top of Long's small desk.

'Mrs Pearlie, are you a colleague of Agent Williams?' he asked. 'I thought there were no women in the FBI. It's about time Hoover joined the twentieth century.' He grinned at me and winked so I'd know he was teasing.

'I'm from another agency,' I said. 'The Office of Price Administration.'

'Sure you are,' he answered. 'Do you two mind if I smoke?'

When we shook our heads he pulled out a crushed pack of Marlboros from his desk drawer and lit it with a Victory match.

'Two smokes a day,' he said, puffing away. 'That's all my doctor lets me have. I punctured a lung in the same shoot-out that messed up my leg.' He blew the match out and pinched the hot tip before flipping it into a trash can.

'It would have been better for you to have hailed from a different government office, Mrs Pearlie. The folks around here are good Americans, but they don't take kindly to the government telling them what prices to charge for the fruits of their labor, if you get my drift.'

'So I have discovered!'

Williams was getting impatient with our bantering, shifting from foot to foot. He didn't understand that we country people sounded each other out by bouncing small talk off each other. Long might be elderly and lame, but his mind was sharp, and I doubted he was afraid of anyone, as Williams had suggested earlier.

'Were you able to find answers to any of the questions we talked about, Officer?' Williams asked.

'Some,' Long said. 'You asked about Leroy Martin. Yeah, I've heard stories that he drives around at odd hours of the night, and I know he's been buying black market gasoline . . .'

'Who from?' Williams asked, instantly alert.

'There ain't no need for you to know that,' Long said.

'What are you talking about? He's breaking the rationing laws!'

'Course he is,' Long said, shifting in his chair, 'but so what? If you go and arrest the filling station attendant, who the hell are you going to find to take her place? We got just one filling station in town. All the young men are in the Army, and the older able-bodied men, and a lot of the women, work at the naval station or in the oyster cannery where they can make real money. Believe it or not, last year Calvert County had a policeman who could walk. He's in the Pacific now.'

Williams backed down. 'We'll talk about that later,' he said. 'Just tell me if you've ever followed Martin on any of his late night jaunts.'

'Son, we got two law enforcement officers in all of Calvert County. I'm on in the daytime. I go to a different town every day and sit by a telephone. On the weekend I sit by my telephone at home. If someone calls me about a problem I look into it. There's a state trooper on at night. If someone calls him he looks into it. We ain't got the gas to drive around the county following people who might be doing a little off-season hunting to put some meat on the table, or maybe visiting a girlfriend.'

Williams told him about the scene we'd witnessed last night, and how this morning the ferryman—

'That's Dennis Keeler, he's a pal of Leroy's,' Long said.

—had threatened us with a shotgun, and how Mrs Cooke, the farmer's wife, had reacted to Williams when he identified himself as an FBI agent.

'The thing is, Constable,' Williams said, 'what Leroy Martin and the other man were loading onto Martin's truck, it looked an awful lot like a corpse. And the tobacco barn floor was soaked with blood, lots of it. What I want to know is, has anyone around here disappeared?'

Officer Long dropped his rural policeman's pose. His dog sensed the change in him and sat up, fixing her gaze on him intently. Long looked at me for confirmation.

'It sure could have been a corpse,' I said. 'It was heavy enough, and it hung between them like a body. But it was dark, and whatever it was was wrapped in sailcloth, so we can't be sure.'

'I don't like the sound of this at all,' he said. 'Someone is missing from this town, but no one has reported it to me officially. Gladys Cooke's husband, Frank. I've haven't seen him around for a while. Neither has anyone else. The girl at the café asked me had I seen him, because he used to come in for lunch with the crowd from the cannery. Then the girl at the filling station asked about him. And he wasn't at church last Sunday neither. I got concerned enough I went to ask Gladys about it.'

'What did she say?' Williams asked.

'Gladys told me he was working at the naval station on Solomons Island now, and the hours were so long, he was renting a room from someone near the base.'

'Did you check her story out?'

'There weren't no way to check it out,' Long said. 'She didn't know the name of the guy who rented Frank his room. Plus if a wife says her husband ain't missing, I got no business looking for him.'

The whole time Long and Williams were exchanging cop talk I was wondering if all this – Leroy driving around the country at night, bloody goings on at the old tobacco barn at Hilltop Farm, and Dennis Keeler's refusal to cooperate with us, at the point of a shotgun – had anything to do with my job, investigating the peculiar postcard sent from Richard Martin in France to Leroy Martin. Was it a coincidence that while investigating the postcard OSS and the FBI had fallen over some local criminal activity? I couldn't see any relationship between the two issues, no matter how I stretched my imagination. But even if Williams was no longer interested in the postcard from France, I was.

Long rose from his chair, gripping his cane as he moved from around his desk. 'Let's drive out to Gladys's place and talk to her again,' he said. 'Maybe if we all show up there it will loosen her tongue. She must know something about what went on at that tobacco barn last night.'

'I've got to put this vial of blood on the bus to D.C.,' Williams said. 'Before we go out to the farm if I can.'

Long checked his watch. 'The express bus heading north pulls into the filling station in ten minutes. We can make it.'

'Tell you what,' I said. 'You two go on up to the filling station. I'm going to see if Anne is in the library.' If I could talk to Anne without Williams I might be able to get her to open up to me.

Anne was checking in a stack of returned books, flipping to the back jacket of each one and stamping the index card in the little envelope in the back of the book 'returned'.

The library was tiny, but every nook and cranny was stuffed with books. Stacks of books stood in corners, with their spines neatly facing out. Books were crammed sideways on the bookshelves on top of the books already shelved there. I could see that each one had its Dewey Decimal System label on the spine. That was unusual for a small town library.

Anne glanced up when she heard me open the door and paused in her rhythmic stamping. I didn't see any nervousness at all in her face when she recognized me.

'Hi,' I said.

'Hello,' she answered. 'So, where's your driver? Or should I say that FBI agent?'

News got around fast. 'I'm sorry about that,' I said. 'It wasn't my idea. He's full of himself, isn't he?'

'Yes, he is!' she said, and smiled at me.

'Did you know he was a cop when we came by your house?'

'I was pretty sure,' she said. 'And when Dennis Keeler came to breakfast at the café he announced it to the world. Where is he?'

'Off with Constable Long,' I said. 'He's got to put a package on the bus to Washington.'

I pulled up a stool to help her, opening each book to the back jacket so she could stamp the index card.

'You've got a nice collection here,' I said. 'Especially for such a small town.'

'The summer people leave them behind,' she said.

'Are you a trained librarian?' I asked, thinking of the neat labels on every spine.

'Not really,' she said. 'We had a real librarian, but she moved to Baltimore to take care of her grandchildren when her daughter got a job. I took a course at the Washington Public Library so I could fill in. I love books. I wanted to keep the library open, even for just a few afternoons a week.'

'You've always loved to read?'

'Always. Of course, when my grandmother and I arrived in the states, I had to learn to read and speak English.'

'You hardly have an accent.'

'Thanks. My grandmother never did pick it up.'

'It must have been so traumatic, losing your family and moving to a new country.'

Anne paused. 'It was awful,' she said. 'A nightmare. The worse one you could imagine. My father and older brother died fighting. My mother and little brother died from typhoid fever.'

'War is so terrible.'

'But America is a magical place. Safe and free. Everyone was kind to us when we arrived here. When my grandmother died, the woman who owned the boarding house where we lived, her cousin was Bertie Woods' grandfather. He got me a job at the café. I met Leroy there. Marrying him made me an American.'

We'd finished stamping the stack of books. Anne began organizing them on a trolley so she could return them to their shelves in order.

'I know Leroy seems rough, but he is very kind to me,' she said. 'He didn't care that I didn't want children. Or that I won't go to church. I haven't believed in God since my family died, but don't spread that around. Leroy only cares if I'm happy.' She looked up from her work and smiled at me. 'And Leroy's happy as long as I cook him a good dinner. So that's what I do, every single night!'

I found Long and Williams drinking coffee in the café.

'So what did you find out?' Williams asked.

'Nothing,' I said. 'I just made friends with her. For now.'
Williams shook his head. 'Women,' he said.

I ignored him. 'Did you get the package on the bus? What's next?' I asked.

'Yes, I did. We're going out to Gladys and Frank's farm. The constable here has a plan, but he won't tell me what it is.'

We left the warm café and ventured outside. The weather was no longer glacial, but still very cold. I pulled the parka hood over my head and drew on my gloves.

'Let's take my police vehicle,' Long said. 'Then Gladys won't know you're with me right away,' he said to Williams.

The policeman's car was a Chevy, black with a white roof and hood, a stubby red light on top, and chains on all the tires.

Long held the back door open for me.

When we arrived at the farm, Gladys was standing on the porch wrapped in a quilt and smoking a cigarette, held primly between her thumb and forefinger, as if she didn't do it very often. I guessed no one smoked in her house.

'Hello, Constable,' she said as we got out of the police car. 'What can I do for you? You,' she said, staring at Williams and me, 'I got nothing to say to you.'

'I don't like to interfere in someone's private business,' Long said, 'but this has gone on long enough. Agent Williams, will you go on around to the back door and keep watch?'

Gladys started and a scowl crossed her face. She threw her cigarette butt into an empty flowerpot. 'What is this about, Ben?' she asked.

Williams started around the house.

'I'm looking for Frank,' Long said.

'He's not here. I told these two that. He's working at the base.'

'Can we come in?'

'Does it matter what I say?' she said.

Once inside, Long glanced at me and then nodded at the

staircase. 'Mrs Pearlie, would you be so kind as to search the second floor? There are three bedrooms and a bathroom. Don't worry, Frank won't harm you.'

'Ben, I told you . . .!'

'Enough, Gladys, I know he's here somewhere. You might as well tell me where, before Agent Williams gets all FBI on us and shoots him.'

I was halfway up the stairs when Gladys answered Long.

'Oh, all right! I warned him, I did!'

Frank was hiding in the kitchen pantry, seated on the floor between a tub of flour and a butter churn. Long hauled him to his feet. Williams joined us in the kitchen, shoving his gun back in its holster.

'What is going on here, Frank?' Long asked.

'I was taking a nap,' he said, '"til Gladys woke me up and told me you were coming up our hill, and not alone.'

'That was stupid,' Long said. 'Makes you look guilty.'

'Guilty of what?' Frank said.

'Of whatever you and Leroy Martin were doing down at your old tobacco barn last night,' Long said. 'Reckon that's why you needed a nap.'

'Weren't doing nothing wrong,' Frank said, sullen.

'So why did you conceal yourself from us this morning?' Williams asked.

'Because I didn't want to talk to you, that's why. Government people, you got to poke around in everyone's business! I got two days off because I worked on the weekend at the base, and I don't want to spend it with you!'

Gladys stood by, not saying a word, with her arms crossed. She was annoyed, but I couldn't tell if it was with us or with her husband.

'Lying to the FBI is a bad idea,' Long said.

Frank shrugged.

'Mr Cooke,' Williams said, 'there was a lot of fresh blood in that tobacco barn. It looked like there was murder done.'

Frank acted as if he'd been shot. His mouth gaped open in shock. He grabbed onto the back of a kitchen chair to steady himself.

Gladys gasped. 'Frank, what are they talking about!'

'Murder!' he said to Long. 'Are you crazy?'

'You and Leroy Martin carried something bloody, the size of a person's body, wrapped in sailcloth, out to Leroy's truck and drove off with it,' I said, 'and crossed the Patuxent on Dennis Keeler's ferryboat, which had no business out on a frozen river at that time of night.'

Frank's face had frozen into the shape of an 'O'. He seemed physically unable to speak. Gladys had collapsed into a chair and was fanning herself with a kitchen towel.

Long turned to Williams and me. 'Agent Williams, Mrs Pearlie, would you kindly excuse us? I'd like to speak with Frank and Gladys alone.'

It was time for Agent Williams to be shocked. 'Absolutely not!' he said.

'I might remind you, Agent, that you are a guest in my county. You are out of your jurisdiction. I'd appreciate it very much if you and Mrs Pearlie waited for me in the car.'

I took Agent Williams by the arm and pulled him toward the front of the house. He was too astonished to resist.

Once outside on the porch he collected himself and turned to go back inside.

I took his arm again, this time more gently. 'Look,' I said. 'Constable Long knows these people. Maybe for their whole lives. Let him talk to them.'

Agent Williams wasn't stupid. He saw the reason in what I said. We went on out to the car and waited for Long.

He came out alone and slid into the front seat.

'Well?' Williams said.

'Well what?' Long answered, turning the ignition.

'Did they tell you anything?'

'Yeah, they did. But it's nothing that you need to know.'

'There might have been murder done!'

'There was no murder,' Long said. 'I promise you that. In fact, I don't think there's a thing going on here that an FBI agent would be interested in.'

'Listen, Long—!'

'That's Constable Long to you,' the constable said, shifting into gear. 'I'm going to find Dennis and question him. You're welcome to come, but only if you allow me to do this my way.'

I sat in the back seat and listened to the men wrangle. I had my own issues. Whatever was going on had nothing to do with the postcard to Leroy from Richard Martin, and that concerned me.

I leaned forward and touched Long on the shoulder. 'Constable,' I said, 'would you please drop me off at the café?'

'Why?' Long said.

Williams turned around and stared at me disapprovingly.

'Special Agent Williams and I came to St Leonard on a different matter than this,' I said. 'I don't want to lose track of it.'

'There may have been a serious crime committed here!' Williams said.

'I understand,' I said, 'but I think that you and Officer Long can deal with that. You're law enforcement officers, I'm not.'

'What different matter?' Long asked.

I wasn't going to tell the constable about the postcard from France. He had nothing to do with that.

'I want to talk to Anne Martin again. She warmed up to me this afternoon, and Leroy will be at work. You two deal with Dennis, and I'll talk to Anne.'

'You just talked to her.'

'That was to soften her up.'

I had to give Williams some credit. He looked angry, but didn't say anything in front of Long.

'Can I have the keys, please?' I asked, holding out my hand to Williams.

Now he was startled. 'The keys?' he said.

'The keys to your car,' I said. 'I'm hardly going to walk to Anne's.'

Off the main road, the ice hadn't melted as much as it had in town. In the woods near the Martin cottage, branches, fences, even individual spears of grass, were coated with a shell of ice that gleamed and sparkled, turning the world into a

glistening wonderland. As this was the first time in my life
I'd driven anywhere near ice, I proceeded cautiously on the
roadbed, the chains on the car's back tires gripping what gravel
and crushed oyster shell protruded from the ice. Even so I
nearly slid off the road twice. When I finally arrived at the
Martins' house, I realized my hands were gripping the steering
wheel as if it were a lifeline.

Damn it, Leroy's truck was parked outside the door!
Why wasn't he at work? It was past time for his shift to
begin.

I parked the car in a patch of sun, hoping to keep the interior
warm, and got out. Stillness surrounded me. Except for the
cracks of tree branches breaking under the weight of the ice,
I heard not a sound.

I felt the hood of Leroy's truck as I passed by it on my way
to the front door. It was cold, hadn't been driven today. And
there was just a trickle of smoke rising from the chimney. The
place felt deserted.

And the front door was ajar. In this weather?

I figured I had two choices. I could retreat to the car and
drive away, find Constable Long and Agent Williams and bring
them back here.

Or I could check the house myself.

I wished I had a gun.

Instead, I removed my switchblade, the one I'd been
issued at the Farm, from my purse and slid it into my coat
pocket.

It was impossible to walk quietly on the path, which was
crunchy with oyster shells and ice. So I decided to call out,
warn whoever might be inside that I was coming in. 'Anne!'
I called out. 'Mr Martin? Is everything all right?'

No one answered me. I pushed the door, and it swung
silently open. I left it that way. I might need to run away,
quickly. I made sure I had the car keys in my coat pocket,
ready to grab.

'Hello! I'm coming in!'

I stepped through the front door and into the small entryway.
Anne's bicycle leaned up against a wall. So where was she?
I called out again. 'Mr and Mrs Martin?' A few seconds

passed. The place felt empty. I pulled out my knife and flicked the blade open.

Inside the kitchen the stove was barely warm; just a few embers glowed when I opened the oven door. I could see into the back room and out one of the windows. There were no birds on the bird feeders. But I did smell iron.

Blood, and plenty of it, soaked the rug under which the body of Leroy Martin lay. It didn't take an FBI agent to see what had happened. He must have died very quickly after the second the oyster knife sliced into his throat.

My heart pounded and blood drained from my head, making me feel lightheaded. I forced myself to think. Quickly, I passed through the sitting room and checked the bedroom and bathroom, methodically opening closets and searching under the bed, even opening a trunk that held blankets. There was no one in the house. I went back to the sitting room and touched Leroy's hand. It was as frigid as the house. He'd been dead a long time.

I located the telephone and lifted the receiver. It was dead. I'd have to drive to town to get help.

But where was Anne?

I called out Anne's name, but still heard nothing but wind and ice cracking as it melted and fell from the trees. Perhaps she had run away?

It didn't make sense that she'd been murdered, too. Why would murderers leave Leroy's body in the middle of the living room floor, but not Anne's? If she'd run, though, they might have left her where she fell, or she could still be running. I prayed that wherever she was she had a coat!

Out the sitting room window I noticed the shed where Leroy kept his gear. The padlock was hanging from its hasp.

I ran out the back door toward the shed. I'm sure I looked ridiculous, crashing across the icy grass, calling Anne's name, clutching an open blade, as if I could fight off whoever had killed Leroy, a powerful man with guns and such to hand.

But I was so afraid for Anne that I ignored all that and made for the unlocked shed. If Anne was alive inside, she would be so terribly cold. She could be injured, too.

A few feet from the door I heard the sounds of muffled screams. Opening the door I saw her. Anne was tied to a framing post with heavy rope and gagged with a scarf. But thank God she had on her coat. When Anne saw me come through the shed door she tried to scream again, but little sound escaped the scarf. I pulled the scarf free, and words mixed with tears tumbled out of her.

'A man came,' she said. 'I was adding crumbs to the bird feeders, and he grabbed me and knocked me down and tied me up in here!'

'Who was he?' I asked, sawing at the thick ropes that bound her. Her wrists were rubbed raw and black where she'd struggled with the bindings until they were loosened, and bruises on her face were forming.

'I don't know. He was behind me. Wearing a scarf, a hat, and gloves.'

Anne gulped in air as I freed her, panting as if she hadn't been able to breathe properly while the scarf covered her face.

'Where's Leroy?' she asked. 'He hadn't left for work yet. Is he all right?'

I pulled her to her feet, where she rocked unsteadily as blood returned to her legs.

'Where's Leroy?' she asked again.

'I'm sorry.'

Anne did as good a job of calming herself as I've ever seen anyone who'd just realized there was bad news. She straightened up and gazed at me with clear eyes. 'He's dead?' she said.

'Yes, I'm sorry.'

'We need to call the police.'

'The phone line is dead. We need to get out of here and get back to town so we can find Constable Long and Agent Williams. And you need a doctor.'

'Please let me see his body.'

I hated to do that, not because I didn't think she could bear it, but because I wanted to get law enforcement on the scene as possible. But I let her go inside.

Anne stared down at Leroy's body. 'You fool,' she said to

his lifeless corpse. 'I warned you. I told you something like this could happen.'

Mrs Lenore Sullivan was one of the kindest women I had ever met. She welcomed Anne like a daughter.

'Honey,' she said, 'you can stay here for a few nights. You shouldn't go back to your house for a while. I'll go make up a room.'

Collins and Williams had left. I'd come down from my own room, where I'd rested while they questioned her. Mrs Sullivan didn't leave the two of us until after she'd stoked up the fire in her sitting room and brought us quilts and hot chocolate. Her dog, Lily, sensing the gravity of the situation, lay quietly at my feet, soothing us with her presence.

Anne's eyes were so ringed with dark circles that it looked like she had two black eyes. She'd spent two hours being grilled by Constable Long in Lenore's sitting room, with Agent Williams in an advisory capacity. And elderly and kind as Long was, I didn't think I'd want to be interrogated by him.

I didn't take part in the FBI's search of Leroy's house or Anne's interrogation. I spent the time in my room napping and taking a long hot bath. We had turned up nothing that indicated any relationship between Leroy's activities or death and Richard Martin's postcard. Richard was a distant relative of Leroy's who just happened to write him about the time Leroy got mixed up in whatever local shenanigans had led to his death. What those shenanigans were no one had explained to me yet.

At this point I was positive there wasn't an 'h' in the word 'St Leonard' after all. The French and British censors had passed the postcard on, and they would know better than us anyway.

I would go back to Washington with Williams early tomorrow and back to work. In the files.

I went into the kitchen for more hot chocolate and found Mrs Sullivan shoving a chicken surrounded by vegetables into the oven to roast.

'You and Anne and Agent Williams are eating here tonight,'

she said. 'If you show up at the café it will turn into a circus. The entire town is riled up.'

'Do you think Anne will be all right?' I asked.

'She'll be fine. Think what she's been through already.'

SEVEN

A lot had happened in the two days I'd been away from 'Two Trees' and my job at the OSS Registry.

When I dropped off my suitcase at home before going to work Wednesday morning I found Dellaphine and Phoebe poring over ration books and recipe pamphlets, trying to unravel the complexities of the new food rationing system.

'Hello there,' Phoebe said to me, when I went to the kitchen to see her before I caught my bus. 'Is your friend better?'

My friend? Oh, of course, Joan, who had a fever, whom I'd been nursing for the last couple of days. My cover story.

'She's fine,' I said. 'Is everything okay here?'

Phoebe gestured at the pile of ration books. 'Trying to make our first grocery list,' she said.

'I don't know how I can be expected to feed you all with two pounds of beef each per week,' Dellaphine said. 'It ain't healthy to eat all that chicken and fish and beans and such.'

'It's so much worse in England,' Phoebe said. 'We'll get by. Do you have time for a cup of coffee, Louise?'

'Yes, please,' I said. 'A quick one.'

The café where Agent Williams and I had stopped for breakfast when we left St Leonard at the crack of dawn had been out of coffee. Retail grocery sales had been suspended until ration books were distributed, and the café owner hadn't planned for it. The tea we'd ordered to accompany our pancakes hadn't cleared my head the way coffee did.

Williams and I had left St Leonard early in the morning so he could file a report with the FBI and request to be assigned to Martin's murder case. Officer Long could not possibly handle it himself, and Williams knew all the principals.

But I'd have nothing to do with finding out who had killed Leroy Martin. I was OSS, and we had no jurisdiction over domestic crime. I hated it. I wanted to know the answers to all the questions I still had about Leroy and Anne.

Williams had told me what he could about the inquiry into Leroy's murder. Anne Martin, questioned by Long and Williams while resting in the lounge of Lenore Sullivan's guesthouse while I was upstairs napping, had implied that Leroy was involved in criminal activity of some kind that had ended in his murder. Wisely, she professed not to know what that criminal activity was, or who Leroy's accomplices were.

Our inquiry into the meaning of the postcard that Leroy Martin received from France was now closed, according to Williams. I had to agree with him. Leroy's death made that moot. The postcard was addressed to him, and from his relative, and if it meant more than it actually said we would never know what that was.

So I had been unceremoniously dropped at my corner with my suitcase.

Before I'd left, Anne had thanked me for saving her life. Which I had, I supposed. If I hadn't gone out to the Martin place, Anne might have frozen in that shed later that night, coat or no coat.

Mrs Sullivan had suggested I return to St Leonard for a nice weekend when the weather was better. I wondered how she would feel if I brought Joe? Just thinking about Joe caused my spirit to lift. Was it the coming weekend we would be together on the houseboat?

My stomach muscles clenched, and a flash of dizziness made me grasp at the kitchen doorjamb for support. I was nervous. How silly! I was a grown woman. I could do as I pleased.

As long as certain people didn't find out about it.

My inbox was stacked inches high with reports and intelligence that needed to be evaluated and filed. I'd expected as much, but I hadn't anticipated the air of overwork and anxiety that permeated the aisles and reading rooms of the Directory. My co-workers barely greeted me as I entered the vast cavern of file cabinets, just nodded and went back to their work.

Ruth passed by my desk with her trolley full of paperwork.

'What's going on?' I asked. I felt that I needed to whisper, it was so quiet.

'The news is bad,' Ruth said. 'Very bad. Convoy ON-166 has been attacked; they've lost fourteen ships in three days.'

Ruth dropped her voice even lower.

'If we can't stop the U-boats, everyone says we're going to lose the war. We can't invade Europe. We can't supply North Africa. We can't locate the U-boats when they are out at sea. Every person here has been assigned to search for targets in Europe that the RAF can bomb that might affect the Kriegsmarine's ability to function. And have you heard about Hans and Sophie Scholl?'

Hans and Sophie were brother and sister, leaders of a German student non-violent resistance group called the White Rose at the University of Munich. They'd been arrested recently for handing out anti-war leaflets and charged with high treason.

'What's happened to them?'

'They were executed, by guillotine.'

No wonder a pall hung over OSS. The student anti-Nazi resistance movement was our best path to infiltrate Germany. Without doubt OSS had been supplying the dissenters; perhaps we even had agents placed in the group. The Scholls' execution was a disaster. Guillotined! I shuddered at the thought of those two young people dying so horribly.

'Any more good news?' I asked Ruth.

'Just don't look at a newspaper,' she said. 'It's scary.'

I walked through the Reading Room on my way to my desk. Every chair was filled. Files crowded the tables, and library trolleys filled all the available space. Men, mostly in uniform, and a few women combed through documents seeking Nazi weaknesses. This railway station, were supplies for the submarines loaded here? That bridge, did supply trucks for submarine bases cross it? Was that building a torpedo factory? Possible targets would be fed to the RAF and American Army Air Force in Britain. Which got their supplies from the convoys. It was a vicious circle that had to be stopped.

I forced myself to forget everything else except my own work. I ploughed through two documents, analyzing and indexing them. Then I took a short break to write a brief report on *l'affaire de carte postale française* to deliver to my boss, Laurence Egbert. He would pass it on to the Foreign Nationalities Bureau.

I gave Egbert a straightforward account of my time in St Leonard and summarized Agent Williams' conclusion that Leroy Martin had been murdered for reasons that had nothing to do with Richard Martin's postcard. I was careful not to criticize Williams, but I did say that I was concerned that the murder of Leroy Martin had obscured OSS's original inquiry about the postcard. Simply because we'd run into a domestic crime didn't mean that there was no meaning to the postcard. I did agree with Williams that there was little that could be done now that Leroy Martin was dead, though.

As I dropped my report off with Egbert's secretary I wondered if I'd ever have another chance to work in the field.

The bustle of the crowd and steady roar of conversation in the OSS cafeteria cheered me up a bit. I didn't see any movie stars today, but I did catch sight of Joan waving her arms at me from a table across the way. Gripping my tray of chicken potpie, milk, and Jell-O, I forced myself through the crowd and slid onto a chair next to her.

'Dearie,' she said, holding my tray for me as I took off my coat, 'it's been as much as my life is worth to hold onto this seat for you.'

'Thanks,' I said, and realized how fond I was of this big hearty woman. She was about the only person in Washington I felt I could talk to without reservation. I needed badly to tell her everything that had happened to me in the last few days, but even the OSS cafeteria didn't offer the privacy I needed.

'So how was your adventure?' she asked.

'Less than adventurous.'

'That's too bad. How come?'

'The company was terrible,' I said, thinking of Williams and his condescension. 'But the guesthouse we stayed in was lovely. We should go there for a weekend when the weather is better. And –' here I leaned into her – 'the subject of our investigations was murdered!'

Joan's mouth dropped. 'You're joking!'

'I am not. But it had nothing to do with our mission,' I said. 'It's the FBI's case now.'

Just as I raised a forkful of pot pie to my lips, an enormous Scotsman knocked my elbow, sending my bite of pot pie splat onto Joan's shirt. I knew he was a Scotsman because of his tartan tam o'shanter. Otherwise he looked like any other British soldier. Then there was his accent, of course!

'Oh, lassie!' the guardsman said to Joan, dismayed. 'I've dirtied your blouse!'

'No worries,' Joan said, 'it will come out,' as she scrubbed at her shirt with a napkin dipped in her water glass.

The two caught each other's gaze and I could feel the current pass between them.

'You take my seat,' I said to the Scot. 'it's time for me to get back to work anyway.'

He didn't object, sliding into the chair I relinquished.

Joan grasped at my arm as I left. 'Meet me after work,' she said. 'Let's get a martini.'

After remembering that it was Wednesday, when Joe was often late getting home, I agreed. 'I really need to talk to you,' I said. 'Could we go somewhere other than a bar?'

The Scotsman had taken my seat by now, and his large body came between me and Joan, who had to lean around him to speak to me.

'I'll pick you up at the corner of G and twenty-first,' she said. 'We'll go to my apartment.'

Joan poured me an ice-cold martini from her sterling silver shaker.

'No olive, right?' she said. 'How about a twist?'

I accepted, watching her carve a sliver of yellow from the skin of a lemon and arrange it on the lip of my martini glass. I sipped from the elegant glass, savoring the sensation of Gilbey's gin rolling down my throat. Thank God for the juniper berry!

I had been raised to believe drinking was a sin. Then I came to the big city and rejected most of my upbringing within months. Okay, weeks! It no longer seemed wicked to me to drink cocktails in a bar, skip church, or date a man I had no interest in marrying just for the fun of it. My poor parents! I hadn't been home to visit since I left North Carolina, and it was getting more and more difficult to write them letters about my life, since most of it would horrify them. They had no idea I worked for a spy agency, lived in a boarding house with male residents, and made more money in a month than my father did in three.

Joan had other lovely possessions to keep company with the silver martini shaker. Like silk pajamas, a mink coat and diamond earrings. Her family had plenty of dough and supplied her with an allowance that let her keep a studio apartment in the Mayflower Hotel. I adored the Mayflower. Much of my first foray into fieldwork involved time spent at the Mayflower. To me the grand hotel felt like a fairytale palace, with its huge crystal chandeliers, frescoed walls, and the three-story ballroom where I'd gone to my first formal affair, a USO gala. I'd eaten twice at the Presidential Restaurant where the movers and shakers of Washington lunched every day.

My dream was to keep working after the war and get my own apartment and car. Or go to college. Not to remarry. Which was what I was supposed to want more than anything, a second husband who made a good living. I just didn't. Despite the war, or maybe because of it, I was happier than I had ever been in my life.

'You're not listening,' Joan said. 'You're ruminating! What about?'

'Oh, I'm sorry! I was thinking about, well, how good, in a way, the war has been for me.'

'Me, too,' she said.

'You?' I was surprised.

'Dearie, I was so bored, I cannot tell you. Keeping house for my father, the Junior League, tennis and swimming. I was doing all the things I was supposed to, but the days went by so slowly.'

Joan didn't mention her biggest disappointment, that she didn't have a husband. So I asked the obvious question. 'What happened between you and the Scot today?'

'His name is Andrew McRoberts. It was too loud to talk

much, but he did ask for my phone number. And what about you? Seeing anyone?'

She immediately saw the indecision on my face.

'Not that professor from Czechoslovakia? We've talked about this. You shouldn't – he's a foreigner. Do you know any more about him?'

'No. But I don't care.'

Joan shook her head. 'Well,' she said, 'you're a widow, so you can get away with dating someone mysterious, I suppose.'

'Since I don't need to protect my virginity?'

'You can make fun if you want. But it's a serious thing for an unmarried woman. And for OSS staff with Top Secret clearance.'

'Joe taught in England for years. And your Scot has an accent.'

'It makes a difference if it's not British, dearie.'

The bus I caught home dropped me at the Arts Club on 'I' Street, just a block from my boarding house. As I crossed the street I stepped onto a two-foot wide swathe of discarded chewing gum frozen into a slick patch. My feet went completely out from under me, and I landed hard on my fanny, knocking the breath out of me. I gasped like a dying fish in the middle of the dark street, gazing powerless at the headlights coming right at me, when someone grasped me under the arms and pulled me onto the sidewalk.

It was Joe, of all people.

'Are you all right?' he asked. 'You took quite a tumble.'

The car that had been about to run me down went past, way faster than the wartime speed limit, and on ice, too.

Fool.

'Thank you!' I said to Joe. 'You got here in the nick of time. Where did you come from?'

Joe grinned at me. 'We were on the same bus. I was rows behind you, too far back to speak to you. I thought I'd surprise you when I got off at the back door.'

'You surprised me all right,' I said. 'And you might have saved my life. That car was coming up fast.'

'He saw you,' Joe said, brushing off my coat. 'I saw his

eyes. Avoiding you would have sent him up on the sidewalk though, fast as he was going.'

Joe glanced down at the packed hard layer of chewing gum that stretched from the curb out into the street. 'Sometimes I just don't understand Americans. What a filthy habit! And if you must chew gum, why not discard it properly?'

Without thinking I rubbed my bottom, which was smarting from its contact with the street.

'Here,' Joe said, 'let me.' He led me deep into an alley and took me in his arms, gently stroking my bruised hip with one hand while holding me tightly against him with the other. His lips found mine, and we stood there locked together for I don't know how long. I can't pretend I felt much, cold as it was, but my imagination was certainly stimulated, and I remembered it would be just a few days until we'd be together on a houseboat, alone, on the Potomac River. Where we'd be very warm and could feel every inch of each other's body. A few days!

I felt panic hit me, and I pulled away.

'Something wrong?' Joe said, releasing me.

'No, no, of course not,' I said. 'I just need to catch my breath.'

'Of course,' he said. 'And it's freezing. It's supposed to be warming up, but I don't believe it. Have you eaten anything?'

'Not yet,' I said. And I'd had two martinis at Joan's. Maybe that explained why my stomach was turning cartwheels.

'We'd better head home,' Joe said. He paused for a minute and kissed me on both cheeks, sweetly. 'You're still okay with going away with me this weekend, aren't you?' he said. 'You can change your mind, you know.'

'I'm not going to change my mind,' I said. But I realized that I almost wanted to. Why? I didn't understand my own feelings anymore.

We slid all the way back to 'Two Trees', holding hands. We only took a tumble once. Joe slipped, and I fell right on top of him, and the two of us skidded along the sidewalk like a sled with a passenger hanging on for dear life. We laughed so hard that we could barely get up. Finally, Joe grabbed at a fence and pulled himself to his feet, and I sort of climbed up him.

'We're going to be covered with bruises tomorrow,' he said.

We made it to our boarding house without further incident. Inside it was toasty warm, at least downstairs, and welcoming. We pulled off our coats and went down the hall to the kitchen, ravenous, where we found that Dellaphine had saved us fried chicken and biscuits with honey, which we chased with glasses of cold milk.

The kitchen was empty, except for the two of us having our supper at the kitchen table. A domestic scene straight from a woman's magazine, I thought, except that I hadn't cooked the fried chicken and Joe and I weren't married. Which was fine by me! Shocking, I thought, that a thirty-year-old widow with glasses wasn't desperate for a husband. What else about me would change before the war was over?

Joe pulled a folded section from a newspaper out of his coat pocket. 'Listen,' he said, 'tomorrow night is the last time the Park Service is going to allow skating on the Reflecting Pool. Want to go?'

'I can't ice skate! I grew up in North Carolina!'

'You can roller skate, can't you?' he said. 'I'll help. Skating on the Reflecting Pool might be a once in a lifetime opportunity. And you can rent skates there. Let's do it.'

'Okay,' I said.

'Can you meet at the west end of the pool? About six thirty?'

'Sure.' Why not? Ice skating in the moonlight in front of the Lincoln Memorial – yet another new experience to add to my wartime adventures.

OSS forbade its staff to keep journals or diaries. I expected I would regret that someday. How could I remember all the little bits of my new world that crowded on me every day? Oh, I could never forget my first paycheck, the day I swore my oath and pressed my inky fingers onto my OSS fingerprint card, the first time I had dinner alone with a man whom I hadn't known since I was a child. I wondered if I would lose the little things, though, like making a war cake without butter or sugar, crowding onto the steps of the Water Gate for a concert, or trying to make a spool of thread last for three dress hems and a pocket repair. I think that's when I first thought of it – as soon as the war was over I'd sit down with a notebook and list everything, every tiny item, I could remember. And I resolved to add new mementos to the shoebox in my closet to join the tickets, photos, and letters already tucked away there.

Joe washed our few dishes while I had a cup of tea. I thought I would never get over seeing a man working at the kitchen sink!

Joe retired to the lounge and its blazing fire with the evening newspaper. I wiped the stickiness off the honey pot at the sink and restored it to its place in the pantry.

I noticed the newspaper clipping when I closed the pantry door. It had been thumbtacked to the wood, its headline underlined in black ink.

'Common Mistakes Regarding China and Japan,' it read. I'd seen the article before. It was an advertisement from *Life* magazine placed in the *Washington Post*. What the government called white propaganda, probably written by our own Morale Operations Division. Posting the clipping here was Henry Post's doing, no doubt. He was always eager to broadcast his political opinions.

I read the article through. According to *Life* magazine, it was understandable that a decade ago Americans believed the Japanese people were like us. They seemed progressive, efficient and modern. Japanese trains ran on time and their best hotels were as luxurious as ours.

The Chinese, in contrast, were subsistence farmers or simple craftsmen. Chinese trains rarely ran on time, and their guest accommodations were barely adequate. The Chinese seemed as un-American as could be.

But, *Life* continued, the 1937 Japan-China war exposed the Japanese as they really are – brutal, arrogant, ruthless in their quest for power. And the Chinese revealed themselves to be kind, self-sacrificing and prepared to give their lives for freedom. Just like us Americans.

According to *Life*, after the war China would evolve into the great democracy of the East. It was our job, as freedom-loving Americans, to support them by sending the planes, tanks, trucks and big guns they required so they could keep the Japanese at bay.

I suppose this kind of propaganda kept Americans working beyond their limits to win this enormous, terrifying war. But working at OSS had taught me to look at the world not in black and white, but in shades of gray. I was party to more war information than the average American, even if I did pick much of it up in the ladies' restroom and the OSS cafeteria.

The Japanese military government ruled Japan, keeping its foot firmly on the necks of superstitious Japanese peasants who thought their Emperor was a god. If we were successful at defeating them, as we must be, what would those people be capable of becoming?

And the Chinese harbored more than one revolutionary movement. The Reds, supported by Russia – which was our ally too, of course – were decidedly undemocratic. We weren't supposed to be worried about this yet.

It was the quiet conclusion of our scholars at OSS and their colleagues at the State Department and in Great Britain that sorting national relationships out after the war would take years.

I suppose what bothered me most about the article was the photographs that accompanied it. Why did the common representation of the Japanese man, with his hair neatly parted and slicked, round glasses, and small mustache, look so sinister? While the elderly Chinese man, lined and white-bearded, wearing a simple skullcap, seemed so kind and unthreatening.

And, of course, the United States had its share of Chinese-Americans and Japanese-Americans, who were being treated by their fellow citizens according to these stereotypes.

I couldn't think about great national issues any more tonight. My brain hurt. I was going to fill my hot water bottle, dash upstairs into my cold bedroom, don my long underwear, flannel pajamas and knit cap and dive into my bed.

The next morning I found a note from Lawrence Egbert, my boss, on my desk asking me to come by his office as soon as I arrived. He'd read my report and wanted to discuss it with me.

My heart pounding, I wound through the stacks of files and

desks until I got to his office, a glass-enclosed cubicle along the front wall of the Registry. I could see him through the window, standing at a table stacked with documents, talking to a man I didn't know. Actually, he was shaking his head more than talking, holding a handful of the yellow slips of paper that requested files from researchers in our reading rooms. The second man in the office shrugged and gestured wide with his hands. Egbert nodded at him again, a sort of 'do your best' kind of acquiescence, pushed the forms into his hand and opened the door for him to leave.

Egbert saw me and raised his eyebrows at his secretary, who sat outside his office.

'This is Mrs Pearlie, sir,' she said.

'Oh, of course,' he answered. 'Come in please, Mrs Pearlie.'

Egbert leaned back against his desk and crossed his arms. 'I found your report to be informative and professional,' he said, 'and I quite appreciate your conclusion that the questions we and the Foreign Nationalities Branch had about the postcard from Mr Richard Martin to his cousin in Maryland have not been answered. But it's not possible for me to continue your assignment.'

That was short and sweet. I had expected it, but still was disappointed.

'You are one of our best indexers,' Egbert said. 'Do you know how many documents we received last month that needed to be read, summarized, and indexed?'

'About ten thousand, sir?'

'Over twelve thousand. If they aren't indexed quickly, competently, and filed, they aren't available to the agencies that need them. We have only fifty-seven indexers to handle this volume. More help just isn't coming anytime soon.'

'I understand,' I said. I did. I knew the Registry's work was critically important.

When I sat down at my desk again, before I set about summarizing and indexing the stacks of raw intelligence piled on my desk, I took the time to scribble some notes to myself about our aborted investigation into Richard Martin's postcard from France, from very near where the Allies were concentrating their efforts to damage what they could of Nazi submarine warfare capability.

I still had the same questions about Martin's postcard I'd had when I first read it. Why spend the money to send such an unassuming epistle to a relative who barely remembered you? Why mention Anne Martin's birthday? Who was 'Mother'?

Then it hit me. I had never verified Anne's birthday!

Yes, it was mentioned on the postcard. Yes, she had affirmed that February thirteenth was her birthday. But had I ever seen documented proof that it was her actual birth date? If it wasn't, would that mean the date had some strategic significance after all?

Not verifying the date of Anne's birthday was a dreadful mistake on my part. I was in charge of the initial research into the postcard. If anyone, for any reason, read this file and noticed this omission, I would look incompetent! I had to find verification of Anne's birthday before I closed the file. If there was no verification, I must inform Egbert immediately.

Perspiration drizzled down my spine and my head spun. I had to put my head down on my desk and think.

Everything would be okay. Here I had access to documents from around the world. I could find the proof I needed. At the worst, Anne herself could probably help me. I didn't want to ask her, though – the fewer people who knew about my negligence the better!

I tore up my notes into tiny pieces and dumped them in the metal trashcan at my feet. The contents would be incinerated at the end of the day. I focused on my regular work.

Later, as dusk dimmed the light coming through the tall glass windows of Registry, I returned to the files of the Foreign Nationalities Branch, where I'd first found evidence of the Martins – Anne's letter identifying herself as foreign born but a naturalized American citizen due to her marriage to Richard Martin.

And here her letter was again, attached to the FNB form that briefly stated she was of no strategic value to the Branch. I was correct. Anne had attached a copy of her marriage license to her letter, but there was no copy of her birth certificate.

That didn't mean she didn't have proof of her birth, just that she hadn't sent it with her letter to FNB. With my magnifying glass and the full light of my lamp directed on the license, I could just see a word in the birthdate space on the license, but couldn't decipher it.

Maybe some proof of Anne's birth date was filed with her marriage license application, which I assumed she completed at the courthouse in Prince Frederick, the county seat of Calvert County. I'd driven through it several times on my way to and from St Leonard. I remembered the courthouse well. It was an imposing brick building with white pillars and a cupola that stood in the middle of a square dominated by elegant oak trees.

How could I search the marriage license records there? No way I could leave OSS, and the courthouse would only be open during regular business hours.

'You're about a million miles away,' Ruth said, pushing her file cart, which must feel like part of her body by now, next to me.

I squeaked and jumped, my hand over my heart.

'Sorry,' Ruth said, 'but I've got to get this load done before I can leave. And I'm tired. As it is I'll miss my quarter-of-a-pound hamburger patty shaped like a T-bone at my boarding house tonight, and have to fill up on mashed potatoes.'

Ruth looked less and less like the Mt. Holyoke girl she was, except that she still wore her pearls every day. Instead of silk she dressed in serviceable suits and a wardrobe of oxford shirts.

She pulled open a file drawer and with gloved hands and taped fingers flew through her filing.

'So how was your time away from the office?' she asked.

'Not very productive,' I said. 'And Egbert said he needed me here. But there are a couple of leads I'd still like to follow up.'

'I wouldn't expect anything else of you,' she said.

'I need to get into the records of the Calvert County Courthouse,' I said, 'but I know I can't get off work again any time soon.'

Ruth stretched, bending backwards with her hands on her

hips. 'Sometimes I wonder about you, Louise,' she said. 'Just call the clerk of court in Calvert County on the telephone. Marriage licenses are public records.'

Of course. I must be more tired than I realized.

I glanced at the twenty-four-hour Navy clock that hung on the wall. Six o'clock. The courthouse would be closed now.

'I'll call first thing in the morning,' I said.

I sat on the edge of the Reflecting Pool, which stretched between the Lincoln Memorial and the Washington Monument, waiting for Joe. The Pool was two thousand feet long and almost a hundred and seventy feet wide, but not an impressive sight, certainly not what its designers had planned. Temporary government buildings from World War One, ugly structures which should have been demolished years ago, squatted on the north side of the Pool, where a parking lot had once stood. Newer buildings nicknamed 'tempos', dormitories and offices, had been built for this war. They ranged around the south side of the Pool. Roosevelt was said to have ordered them to be so flimsy and unattractive that they would have to be bulldozed after the war, rather than left to ruin the area as the World War One buildings had. Two covered pedestrian bridges spanned the pool to link the World War One and World War Two buildings. The buildings were separated from the pool by tall chain link fences with gates, the sort you would find surrounding a factory.

The best place to get on the ice was from the steps of the Lincoln Memorial, where I now sat waiting for Joe. Enough light leaked from the 'tempos' despite blackout curtains and from a quarter moon to illuminate the scene. Lincoln himself sat in shadow. Figures silhouetted against the ice moved gracefully – well, some of them were graceful – across the length of the Pool. The scene, if you ignored the 'tempos', was really quite lovely, like watching a waltz under the night sky.

Joe sat down next to me, ice skates dangling from his hands. He immediately took me in his arms and kissed me, and I felt the warmth of him all the way into my toes.

'Two more days,' he whispered into my ear, and I knew he meant that on Friday night we'd be alone together in his friend's houseboat. Completely alone. Not just somewhere where no one recognized us, but alone. In bed.

I felt myself shudder, and buried my head in his shoulder. I sniffled back tears.

'I'm so sorry,' Joe said. 'Did I embarrass you?'

'It's all right,' I said.

'Here,' he said, quickly changing the subject, 'try these skates on. I rented them from that fellow over there on the bottom step of the Memorial.'

I looked at the fellow. He stood bundled up like an Eskimo, with dozens of pairs of ice skates piled at his feet.

The skates Joe picked out for me appeared to fit. Joe laced his up, then mine, so snugly that I had no wiggle room at all.

'They're so tight,' I said.

'They have to be, to hold your ankles rigid.'

Joe helped me stand, and I've never felt so clumsy in my life. My feet splayed in all directions. Joe had to hold on to me to keep me from falling flat.

'My God,' I said. 'I'll never be able to do this.'

'Sure you will,' he said. 'Sit for a minute and watch me.'

I sat and watched. He skated in a simple figure eight in front of me, his hands behind his back, smiling, and I again thought of how little I knew about him. He could be anyone. But wasn't that part of what attracted me to him? Where I grew up we knew everyone's kin for generations back. Here in Washington we were all strangers.

'Okay,' he said, stopping in front of me and reaching out for my hands. 'Let's go. If we can make it all the way down to the Washington Monument I'll buy you a hot dog at the Park Service concession.'

'What better inducement could there be?' I asked.

Joe wrapped his arms around me, and I held on tightly. Slowly, we skated toward the Monument. I only fell once. And eventually I learned to enjoy the smooth, gliding sensation of my ice skates moving over the ice, and the romantic feel of moving in tandem with Joe. We passed couples, groups of laughing government girls, soldiers trying to pick them up, and the occasional park ranger policing, looking for drunks.

'Lots of people here tonight,' I said.

'It's the last night the Park Service is keeping the Pool open for skating,' Joe said. 'It's warming up again.'

Thank God. When we'd opened the vent between floors last night, Ada and I were both able to bathe without chattering.

We reached the Washington Memorial end of the pond. I noticed a crowd gathered around the concession stand. The sizzle of hot oil filled the air.

'How many dogs do you want?' Joe asked.

'Two, with relish and onions,' I said.

'Sit down and rest your ankles,' he said. 'I'll be right back.'

My ankles burned with the unfamiliar stress of balancing on ice skates. I'd need to take aspirin in the morning for sure. I rubbed them hard.

'First time skating?' a man said to me, skating up and stopping expertly on the toe kick of one figure skate. It was Art Collins from the Foreign Nationalities Branch, my first partner in the mystery of the French postcard. It sounded like a Nancy Drew novel now.

'Yes,' I answered him.

'So,' he said, 'how did things turn out in St Leonard?'

'You know I can't talk about that here,' I said. 'You can find my summary in the files at work.' I felt my heart catch. What if Collins noticed I hadn't verified Anne Martin's birth date? I was sure he would report it to Egbert.

'You know,' Collins said, sitting down next to me, 'you could have been kinder when you reported on our inquiry to Egbert. You knew I was inexperienced.'

I chose my words as carefully as I could. I didn't want Collins to be my enemy. 'I wasn't unkind,' I said. 'I just stated the facts as I saw them.'

'And I went back to my desk and you went back into the field with an FBI agent,' he said.

'Your boss said he couldn't spare you,' I answered.

Collins pulled a pack of cigarettes out of his pocket and lit one with a standard GI black crackled Zippo lighter. 'Would you like one?' he asked, gesturing with the packet.

'No, thanks.'

'I thought you came from tobacco growing country.'

'I do, but smoking makes my throat sore.'

Collins shrugged, inhaled, and exhaled smoke and cold vapor.

Joe sat down on the other side of me, his hands full of a brown bag with grease spots and two cups of hot coffee.

'I could only get us one hot dog each,' he said, 'they're beef, so they're rationed. But I've got French fries with lots of catsup for you and vinegar for me.'

The steam from the hot food filled the air with the odor of meat and potatoes cooked in oil.

I introduced the two men. 'Joe,' I said, 'this is Lieutenant Collins. We work in the same office.'

'Glad to meet you,' Joe said, reaching out his hand.

The sound of Joe's accent had brought Collins instantly to the alert, and he looked at me with speculation in his eyes.

'You're not an American,' Collins said to Joe, though his eyes were fixed on me.

'No, I'm not,' Joe said. 'I'm Czech, but I have a British passport.'

'Really. Why aren't you in the British Army, then?'

No one else but me would have noticed Joe stiffening.

'I was too old when the first soldiers were conscripted. I came to the United States to teach Slavic languages at George Washington University.'

'I see,' Collins said, climbing to his feet easily, despite still wearing ice skates, and pitched his cigarette stub onto the marble of the Monument.

'Maybe I'll see you at the office tomorrow,' he said to me.

'Maybe.'

He turned and gracefully skated back down the Reflecting Pool towards the Lincoln Memorial.

'Sorry,' I said to Joe. 'We worked together on a project, and he didn't like what I said about him in my report. He's inexperienced, and my being a woman wasn't helpful to his ego I suppose.'

I had a feeling that Collins would like to get back at me somehow.

The hot dogs and French fries tasted wonderful. I loved homemade French fries with the skins still on. We didn't have those in North Carolina often. Our potatoes were usually mashed or mixed with Duke's mayonnaise and onions in potato salad.

After finishing our hot dogs Joe dumped the trash into a flaming incinerator.

'Can you skate back down the length of the Pool?' he asked.

'Sure,' I said, 'as long as you hang on to me.'

As we glided – well, Joe glided, I staggered – back down the Reflecting Pool, I saw Joan surrounded by a group of friends, including the Scot from the cafeteria, having a swell time. I suspected it wasn't hot cocoa in their paper cups. She caught sight of me and waved, but when she saw Joe, her brow furrowed. Damn it! Joan too. I was getting tired of this. Washington was full of foreigners and refugees. Why should Joe be treated any differently?

We reached the end of the Pool, and I sat gratefully down on the edge. Joe unlaced his skates and then mine, returning them to the entrepreneur who'd rented them to him. After the skates were off my feet I felt strangely shaky when I stood up, so Joe put my arm through his.

'Let's get a taxi,' Joe said. 'Your ankles are going to hurt more than you know in the morning.'

'It's so expensive, though!'

'It's not far,' he said.

Back home everyone was already upstairs in their bedrooms, though it wasn't quite ten o'clock yet.

'Shall we warm up in the lounge before we go upstairs?' Joe asked.

Ordinarily, I would have jumped to spend time alone with him. Instead I recoiled – not visibly, thank God, but emotionally. I was so surprised by my response that I had to grip the stair banister for support.

'It's late,' I said, glancing up the staircase.

A flicker of disappointment showed in Joe's eyes, then disappeared. 'You must be very tired,' he said.

'Yes, I am.'

Hand in hand we went up the staircase until we reached the first landing, where we'd part: me to my second-floor bedroom, and Joe to climb another flight to his third-floor attic room.

He leaned over and kissed me, his soft beard caressing my cheek.

'Tomorrow we'll be together all night,' he said softly into my ear. 'I'm living for it.'

'Me, too,' I said, as my knees turned to jelly. Oh my God, it was tomorrow! Our first weekend in the houseboat!

Later, when I lay awake in the deep cold dark, clutching my pillow as if it was a life preserver, I faced the truth. I wasn't just nervous about having an affair with Joe. I was afraid.

Despite Joe's affection for me, and mine for him, I was alone in this little escapade. No one would care that he was shacked up with me. But I . . . I was terribly vulnerable.

I depended on my job for everything that had become vital to me. My independence, my own money, never living in my parents' back bedroom ever again.

I never had to marry again if I didn't want to. I made my own decisions.

But I was a government girl with Top Secret clearance at the Office of Strategic Services, America's spy agency, involved, even if sometimes my work seemed deadly dull, with critical espionage documents. If it was known that I was having an affair with a Czech refugee I could lose my job.

Joe's work with the Joint Distribution Committee, a Jewish charity that struggled to help European Jews survive and escape the tragedies that overwhelmed them, had once been legitimate and overt. But since war had been officially declared, all Allied companies and organizations had been forbidden to operate in Europe. So the JDC was now a covert agency too.

If Collins decided to 'report' my relationship with Joe to OSS, I couldn't help but think my new life would be over. I could probably explain a friendship with a fellow boarder, but not an affair. Sex and love raised the possibility of pillow talk, blabbed secrets, or even blackmail.

And I was expendable. Just another government girl. One who sometimes fooled herself that she could work in the field successfully. Who tried to find danger in a simple innocuous postcard so she could stay out of an oppressive file room for another day or two. Who'd alienated two men who would undoubtedly be considered more valuable than she was.

No wonder I was frightened.

EIGHT

I waited on a corner for Joe, about halfway to his office but out of my way. I'd ducked out of the house early, pleading the need to get to my office, so that I could intercept him here.

I spotted him immediately in the crowd of war workers streaming east, despite the fact that everyone was bundled up to their eyebrows in scarves and hats. Joe had one of those fur hats that I called a 'Cossack' hat, with flaps that covered his ears. It looked like his grandfather had herded sheep in it, it was so old and moth-eaten. That hat, a deeply creased leather briefcase and cheap resoled shoes were important parts of his threadbare professorial cover story.

'Good morning,' I said, reaching out to him and taking his arm.

'Why, Louise,' he said, taking my arm in his, 'what on earth are you doing here?'

'I need to talk to you,' I said. 'In private.'

'Of course. Let's go into that café, the breakfast rush is over.'

We unwrapped layers of coats, scarfs, and gloves, piled them all on a chair, and ordered coffee.

'I should have thought of this,' Joe said, after the waitress brought us our order. 'We need to plan for tonight. We should leave separately for the houseboat. What time do you think you can get away from work? Should I get us some food, or do you want to risk going out to dinner?'

I managed to keep myself from taking both his hands in mine. 'Darling Joe,' I said, 'I'm not coming.'

He flinched as though I had struck him, and I felt tears welling up behind my eyes.

He searched for an explanation that wouldn't be painful. 'Something's come up,' he said. 'Work. You've got to go out of town again. I understand.'

'No. I've decided, well . . .' I forgot my speech, and could only squeak out, 'I can't be with you like that.'

'Louise, darling,' he said, 'I'm not free to marry, we've talked about this.'

'You think I'm trying to pressure you into marriage? You think I would do that? I don't want to get married either.'

'Then what has happened?'

I told him, and there was no way to avoid the harsh truth. I cared more about protecting my job and my new life in Washington than consummating our love affair.

'You've given this a lot of thought,' he said.

'If only I could have you and feel safe,' I said. 'But I can't. I can't bear the thought of going back to the way my life was before the war.'

'I see. You came to this conclusion rather late, didn't you? You couldn't have decided this a few weeks ago?'

'When we ran into Collins last night ice-skating is when I first realized the chance I was taking. The man dislikes me and would like revenge. And there might be others.'

Joe leaned his head back and stared at the ceiling. 'I'm taking a risk, too,' he said, 'in my work. We do so much that's illegal now.'

'But what would happen to you if an affair became public?' I said.

'I expect I would get transferred to the New York office. Or maybe Lisbon.'

'Exactly. You would be transferred. I could be fired.'

I was speaking normally, but tears trickled hotly down my cheeks. Joe wasn't crying, but he looked stricken, and dark shadows cut deeply into his face.

'Fine,' he said. And then he got up and left. Leaving me alone.

I waited until I was sure he was on his way, sipping at the bitter dregs of my coffee. My eyes stung from the effort to keep from crying.

The waitress stopped by our table with the bill. 'He's not worth it, honey,' she said.

'Oh, I think he might be,' I said.

I bundled up and left, turning down the nearest alley, almost running to the end of it before spewing onto a pile of filthy ice.

'Are you all right?' Joan asked. She was at the counter, turning in file request slips for General Donovan, when I got to work.

'Not really,' I said. 'I broke it off with Joe.'

'I'm sorry,' she said, 'but it was the right thing to do.'

'Well,' I said, stripping off my coat, scarf, hat and gloves, 'it's done.'

Back at my desk I drew on my fingerless gloves and took the first document from my inbox to read and summarize. It was a complex job, and by the time I was done with my synopsis it took up three index cards.

I went to file the index cards and tossed the document itself on Ruth's cart. Ruth pushed back a straggling hair, her hands heavily bandaged.

'I wonder if I will ever do anything other than this again,' she said. 'I dream about the alphabet at night. Just a year ago my biggest worry in life was if a rich Yale man would invite me to the Heart Ball and whether my mother would let me borrow her sable coat.'

On a quick break I found the one public telephone we were allowed to use and called the courthouse in Frederick, Maryland. It turned out that the chief clerk was a woman who introduced herself as Linda Sundt.

'I'm looking for a marriage license,' I said, 'and whatever supporting documents might be filed with it.'

'I can pull the license for you,' she said, 'but I can't give you any information over the phone. You'll have to come to the office to see it.'

'But I can't,' I said. 'I'm working in Washington.'

'If you can get here tomorrow morning I'll be here. We're on a forty-eight-hour work week now, like the President said, "fight or work".'

Why not? I could drive to Prince Frederick tomorrow morning. I was sure Phoebe would let me use her car. It wasn't like we didn't have jerry cans of gasoline sitting around the garage! I could fill up the car and stash another can in the trunk. It would be good to get out too, instead of moping around the boarding house.

I hadn't thought of what it would be like to live in the same house with Joe now. I wondered if one of us would have to move. It would be almost impossible to find another room in the city. But how could we share space in the house together? I'd need to stay in my cold room by myself.

'I'll do my best to be there tomorrow,' I said.

'I'll pull the file. What's the name?'

'Martin,' I said. 'Richard Martin and Anne Venter.'

'I remember where I know you from,' Agent Gray Williams said.

He was waiting for me outside the door to the OSS cafeteria wearing an OSS visitor's badge.

'Really?' I said. 'I don't remember you.'

'Of course you do,' he said. 'It was last summer. You were dating a man from the Vichy French embassy, and I had to warn you to stay away from foreigners. Don't worry, I don't fault you for not reminding me. It can't be pleasant for a woman to remember her mistakes.'

I felt so worn out and jaded, I didn't even get angry. 'I took your advice,' I said. 'I avoid men with accents at all costs now.'

'Smart girl. Listen, let me take you to lunch. My boss says I can brief you on the Martin murder. We've arrested Dennis Keeler.'

'The ferryman? Has he confessed?'

'Of course not, it's a capital crime.'

Only to hear more about the Martins would I spend another second in this man's company.

We found an empty booth at the café across the street, ordering coffee, open-faced turkey sandwiches with gravy, mashed potatoes and peas. The peas were canned, but the turkey and gravy were hot and tasted homemade.

'Remember when Constable Long insisted we leave the Cooke farmhouse so he could talk to Frank? Well, Frank told him everything. He, Leroy Martin and Dennis Keeler had been smuggling beef to a butcher in Alexandria.'

'Selling it for more than the established price,' I said.

'Exactly. Then the butcher sold the prime cuts for a fortune and disguised the lesser cuts as prime, too. Long didn't tell us because he figured it was a local crime, none of our business. He'd warn them off, and that would be the end of it.'

'Until I found Leroy Martin's body.'

'Yeah, that was something Long didn't expect, for sure.'

Williams gestured for the waitress. 'Do you have any dessert?' he asked her. 'Real dessert, not Jell-O.'

She hesitated. Williams showed her his FBI identification. 'I can find you a slice of coconut cake,' she said.

Williams glanced at me questioningly.

'None for me,' I said. 'I'm not very hungry.'

'Anyway,' Williams said, 'Frank came home from the naval base a couple of nights a week. He and Leroy butchered one of Frank's beeves in the tobacco barn. The FBI lab verified the blood on the floor was bovine, by the way.

'Frank and Leroy dressed the carcass, threw the waste into the Patuxent, loaded up Leroy's truck with the beef, and hauled it to Dennis's ferry landing. Dennis met them and ferried them across the river so they could avoid the main roads. For a price. He wasn't a full partner. Then Leroy and Frank drove the beef to the butcher in Alexandria and both got back home in time for breakfast.'

I drew patterns in my leftover gravy with my fork, until I remembered my table manners and placed it correctly on the side of my plate. Sometimes I wished I could smoke; it seemed to soothe my friends wonderfully.

'There must be hundreds of people doing the same thing all over the country,' I said. 'Mostly obeying the law, but not quite. But they don't murder each other.'

'Ah,' said Williams. 'Here's where the plot thickens. After you found Leroy's body, Constable Long told me what Frank had confided to him. It seems that two of them were considering quitting. Both Leroy and Frank were worried about the strict penalties attached to the new rationing laws. Then, when you and Collins, and then me, showed up at the Martin cottage with questions about the postcard from Leroy's cousin in France, they got really rattled. Not about the postcard itself, but about

all the attention they were getting from the government. Anne
was pressuring Leroy, too.'

'Did Anne know about the smuggling?'

The waitress brought Williams's cake, a big enough piece
for two people. He stabbed at it with his fork.

'She says not, just that she knew Leroy was doing something
he shouldn't. Anyway, Dennis was furious. The money was
so good, and he wanted a bigger piece of the action for himself.
He owned a truck, but it was up on blocks because he didn't
have the money to fix it. Frank told Constable Long that Dennis
was going to ask Leroy for a loan, and then they could double
the business. I figure that Leroy said no, so Dennis killed him.
Maybe he figured he could take Leroy's place.'

In between bites of cake Williams told me the rest of the
story.

While I was discovering Leroy's body and freeing Anne
from the shed, Long and Williams searched for Dennis to
question him about the smuggling operation. He wasn't at
home – in fact his wife was furious because several paying
customers had driven up to the landing who had to be sent
away because her son couldn't operate the ferry by himself.

She directed Williams and Long to Dennis's favorite bar,
but he wasn't there. Nor was he at the café drinking coffee
and griping.

Their search was interrupted when I found Leroy's body
and they were called to the scene. Anne couldn't identify her
assailant; she insisted he had grabbed her from behind and
blindfolded her with her scarf. No, she hadn't noticed his
clothing, or his height, or anything else about him.

Anne wasn't surprised to learn that Leroy had been smuggling
beef, nor that he and Dennis had been arguing over the past few
days. She didn't like Dennis, she said; she felt he was a bad
influence on her husband.

Williams scraped up every last crumb from his cake plate.

'It was Frank who finally found Dennis, in a roundabout
way,' Williams said. 'He saw lights in his old tobacco barn
and called Constable Long. When we got there Dennis was
wrapped up in canvas to keep warm and most of the way
through a bottle of cheap bourbon.'

The waitress cleared our plates and poured us fresh coffee.
'But Dennis says he didn't kill Leroy?'

'He put on a damn good show of being shocked by the
course of events,' Williams said. 'Outraged that we suspected
him just because he and Leroy had argued.'

'Were there any fingerprints on the oyster knife?'

'Nope. Wiped clean. But we'll get the goods on him. Dennis
is not a bright man. He will have made mistakes, and we'll
find them.'

We finished our coffee and turned down refills.

'So you see,' Williams said, 'that French postcard of yours
meant nothing at all. I'm surprised your office bothered, actually. But then they didn't send a real agent.'

I kept my mouth shut. I needed Williams out of my life. I
could take no chances that he would find out about Joe.

Williams threw a few coins onto the table for the tip. 'You're
very competent, Louise. But I expect you'd rather work in the
office than get mixed up in something this disturbing again,
wouldn't you?'

I shook hands with Williams, praying this would be the last
time I ever saw the man, and turned down the street towards
OSS. Before I got there I stepped off into an alley I knew
ended in a tiny park to have a good cry.

I wasn't the only one looking for a private spot.

Seated on a stone bench was a middle-aged man with his
head in his hands. He heard my footsteps and raised his head
from his hands. His face was streaked with tears.

I didn't know what to do. Should I pretend I hadn't seen
him and walk away? I had my own problems. But how could
I do such an unkind thing as walk away from his distress!

He smiled at me wanly, and I pulled my own ravaged heart
together and went over and sat down next to him. The stone
seat was ice cold.

The man wore a checked wool cap and a heavy duffel coat.
A hand knit scarf kept his neck warm. His hair was an ordinary
dirty blond with grey around the temple and ears. In one of
his calloused workingman's hands he held a black-rimmed
telegram.

Oh my God.

'I'm so terribly sorry,' I said. 'Can I help in any way?'

He shook his head. 'Too late for any of that, Ma'am. I'm sorry you had to come upon me like this. I thought I was all right, but then, well, I felt myself giving way and ducked down the alley to compose myself.'

'Your son?' I whispered, feeling my heart clutch.

His eyes welled up again. 'You'd think so, the way I'm carrying on. No, my dog Bonnie.'

For a minute I thought I'd misunderstood him.

'She was such a good dog. My grandchildren adored her.'

'I don't think I understand.' It sure looked like the black-rimmed paper the man held in his hand was an official Army telegram. Perhaps he wasn't quite right in the head.

'When the war started – my name's Alec Newton, by the way – the Army needed more military dogs than they could possibly raise and train from puppies. So they asked citizens to give up their pets, as long as they were healthy and under four years old. They called it "Dogs for Defense". If the dog did well in boot camp, it was in the Army. The washouts went home.'

'So Bonnie . . .?'

'Did real good. Graduated at the top of her class! 'Course, I'd trained her already. She rode with me on my milk truck every day. I couldn't do anything else for the war effort, I'm too old to enlist, got no skills especially. So I gave Bonnie to the Army. Other people willingly sacrificed their sons. The least I could do was donate my dog.'

'She's dead?'

'Yeah, in Greenland. So far away! She patrolled the perimeter of one of our bases there. Here . . .' Newton pulled a crumpled photograph out of his pocket. It showed a young soldier, bundled up like an Eskimo, in a frozen landscape, kneeling next to a small mostly black German shepherd with one floppy ear.

'I got her for free because of that ear,' Newton said.

Bonnie was clothed just as warmly as her soldier. Fur and canvas boots laced up to her knees. A heavy padded canvas coat encased her small body.

'Bonnie's soldier sent me this picture when they first got to Greenland. I hope he's going to write and tell me what happened to her. The telegram just says "in the line of duty".'

The man burst into tears. I put my arm around his shoulder, and before I knew it I was crying uncontrollably with him. The two of us sat together on that cold hard concrete bench and just plain sobbed our eyes out. Not just about Bonnie, of course. About everything else that was so tragic about this awful war.

Newton dried his eyes with his scarf. 'Now I got to tell my wife and daughters and the grandkids.'

'I'm so sorry,' I said, gulping back my own tears. 'You should be so proud of Bonnie.'

'I am,' he said, tucking the telegram and photo away into his pocket. 'I hear the dogs that die in action get a special medal. I hope so.'

I did, too.

I was wrung out when I got home. What had gone on that day had knocked me to my knees more than once. I was on my feet now, but teetering. What I wanted to do was slip upstairs and climb into bed under my covers with my bottle of gin. But I couldn't do that, after what I had done to Joe – I had to face him.

I stripped off my coat, scarf, gloves and hat and threw them over the chair in the hall. Behind me I could hear Phoebe, Ada, and Henry in the lounge. But not Joe's accent. Maybe he wasn't home yet, or was brooding in his room.

Phoebe came out into the hall. 'Louise, I'm so glad you're home! What an awful week it has been. Come sit down by the fire with us. I made cheese straws today, and Henry brought home a bottle of Buffalo Trace. We are determined to be gay!'

I let her lead me into the lounge. A fire was crackling away, and Henry's bottle of bourbon sat open on the cocktail table with Phoebe's best highball glasses. I was right, Joe wasn't in the room.

'You look white as a ghost,' Ada said. 'Here, sit by the fire.' She relinquished the fireside chair, and I sat down. Henry

handed me a glass of whisky, neat. After I had a big swallow
I did feel better.

I couldn't help myself. 'Where's Joe?' I asked.

'Oh, he's gone.'

NINE

I was thunderstruck. I saw in my head clear as day Joe on a train or a ship heading somewhere far away. I'd never see him again.

'For the weekend,' Phoebe said. 'A friend of his lent him his houseboat on the Potomac. He said he just wanted a change of scene.'

Ada took my hand in hers. 'Are you all right?' she asked. 'You just went white as a sheet.'

'No, I'm fine,' I said. 'Just tired.' I took another gulp of whiskey.

'I think the President made a mistake,' Henry said. Henry thought everything Roosevelt did was a mistake. 'Ordering a forty-eight-hour workweek. Exhausted workers make mistakes and become ill.'

I had an opening. 'Phoebe,' I said. 'I was wondering. Could I borrow your car for the weekend? I know it's a lot to ask. I want to go away myself, to a guesthouse on the western shore of Maryland a friend told me about. I'm a good driver.'

I wasn't sure what Phoebe would say. It was one thing for a woman of her generation to let Henry and Joe borrow her car, but might be another to allow me.

'I don't see why not,' Phoebe said. 'Just promise to be home by dark on Sunday? Or I'll worry.'

'Thank you,' I said. 'I promise.'

I called Lenore Sullivan before dinner.

'Yes, dear, of course,' she said. 'I'll be glad to have your company.'

That night, spooning with my hot water bottle in my bed, I planned my strategy. I'd stop at the courthouse in Prince Frederick on my way to St Leonard and verify that Leroy and Anne's marriage license listed her birth date.

Then I'd check in at Lenore's. I planned to stay away from the town itself. I expected it was in an uproar over Leroy's murder and Dennis's arrest and I didn't want to be the center of that kind of public attention. I would go out of town to eat. If I ran into anyone from St Leonard I'd do my best to convince them I was just on a weekend trip because I'd found their town so charming.

When I returned to Washington I'd have the information I needed to complete the Martins' file at OSS and prevent Collins, or anyone else, from criticizing my work.

Then perhaps I could relax in Mrs Sullivan's deep, hot bathtub with my book and try not to think about Joe.

It felt good to be behind the wheel of a car again.

My Daddy taught me to drive his truck when I was fourteen, and of course I drove it back and forth to work when I got my first job at the Wilmington Ship Factory. Here in Washington trying to get anywhere, with the traffic and scarce buses, was a daily frustration. Just putting Phoebe's car in gear and driving out of her garage and turning onto Pennsylvania Avenue was exhilarating. Someday, I swore, I would buy a car of my own.

The streets were still icy in shady spots, and traffic was heavy, since so many people worked on Saturday now, but I had no trouble getting out of town. I had to give Henry some credit. He took very good care of the car for Phoebe, even to the chains he'd carefully fitted to the back tires.

The Calvert County courthouse was busy, as Linda Sundt had said it would be. I found the Records Section in the basement of the courthouse. I felt at home there immediately. It was lined with file cabinets.

I found Linda Sundt behind the service counter, knitting and listening to the radio. She got to her feet immediately, laying the prettiest knitted blanket I think I'd ever seen on the counter. The blanket was a deep periwinkle color with honeycomb cables.

'That is stunning,' I said. I'd tried knitting. I was dreadful at it. I doubted I could even edge this one properly.

'Thank you,' she said. 'My church group makes them for the children's hospitals in England.'

I fingered the thick wool. England was just as cold this winter as we were, but with fewer resources to combat it.

'It was so sad,' Linda said, 'but the last box of blankets we sent was on a ship that was sunk by a Nazi U-boat. It seems like a small thing amongst all the other supplies, and lives, that were lost, but still. It broke our hearts! We're making sweaters now, too, for sale, so we can send money to Great Ormond Street Hospital.'

Sundt lifted a stack of sweaters onto the counter.

Immediately, I pulled one out of the pile. It was a deep blueberry, the same color as my only formal gown. I had to have it. 'I'll take this,' I said.

'Please don't feel like you have to buy one,' she said.

'I don't,' I said. 'I want it. I'm Louise Pearlie, by the way. I called you yesterday?'

'I figured as much,' she said. 'I've got that marriage license you wanted to see. Leroy Martin and Anne Venter?'

'Yes, please,' I said, praying it had the information I needed. While she riffled through her desk I wrote a check for the sweater.

'I'll wrap up the sweater while you look at this,' she said, handing me a folder.

The license was suitably embossed with the state and county seals, filled out with a florid script, and notarized. Anne was listed as Anne Venter, birthplace Orange River Colony, South Africa. But where her birthdate should have been filled in a scrawl read: *birth certificate lost during Boer War, see note.* I turned the license application over and deciphered the handwriting on the back. *Miss Venter produced her baptismal record, dated January 3, 1890, as proof of her birth and nationality.*

That was impossible! It must be a mistake. That was almost six weeks before her supposed birthday in February!

'This can't be right,' I said. 'Anne was born on February thirteenth, 1890. This says she was baptized on January third, 1890.'

Linda took the document from me, carefully reading every

word and the handwritten notations on the back of the certificate.

'I'm sure it's correct,' she said. 'The Clerk of the Court at the time was old Gus Pender. The man never made a mistake in his life.'

'Can I copy it?' I said.

'You make all the notes you want,' she said, handing me paper and pen and motioning me toward a table in the middle of the room.

I copied down every word, so that any visitor to the French postcard file would see that I had been diligent.

But I'd replaced a big problem with one even larger.

Anne had told me that her birthday was February thirteenth, 1890. Now I knew that couldn't be correct. Her baptismal certificate, which the Clerk of the Court of Calvert County had inspected before issuing Leroy and Anne a marriage license, proved that she had been baptized on January third of the same year.

And February thirteenth was two weeks ago. All the questions that worried us at OSS about the Martin postcard surfaced again, unanswered. Why spend so much to send such an innocuous letter to a man who barely remembered you? Why mention 'Mother' to a couple who didn't know Richard Martin's mother? Why refer to Anne's birthday at all?

I needed to talk to Anne again. Perhaps I misunderstood the date she gave me. Maybe she was born in 1889 and wasn't baptized until almost a year later. Somehow I thought that without Leroy present, she would answer all the questions I had and put the matter to rest. I could take my notes back to OSS, stick them in the file, file the bloody thing, and put all this behind me.

I luxuriated in the heat radiating from the potbelly wood stove in Lenore Sullivan's sitting room. Stretched on the lounge, covered with a thick quilt, I managed to read Mary Roberts Rinehart's *Haunted Lady* without thinking too much about either Joe or the Martins. Lily snoozed at my feet.

I was, however, getting distracted by the wonderful aroma coming from Lenore's kitchen. Beef stew, I thought.

Returning to reality made me think of Leroy Martin, Dennis Keeler and Frank Cooke. One man murdered and two in jail because of beef profiteering. And poor Anne widowed!

'I thought you might like to join me in a cup of tea, Louise,' Lenore said. 'I hope you can drink Earl Grey.' She set down a tray with two mugs of steeping tea, a cream pitcher shaped like a cow, a plate of shortbread cookies, and a sugar bowl.

I didn't hesitate. I took a cookie, and I added plenty of cream and sugar to my mug. I sipped the tea contentedly, alternating a slurp of tea with a bite of cookie.

'I hope you'll have dinner with me,' Lenore said.

'I would love to, but I thought you didn't do meals?'

'It's just stew; it's no harder to cook for two than one. And I didn't think you'd want to go into town, what with the murder and all.'

'I'd planned to go out of town to eat.'

'No need to do that.'

'So St Leonard is still talking about the murder?'

'Honey,' Lenore said, pouring a healthy dollop of cream into her mug, 'this town is abuzz with talk about Leroy Martin's murder, Dennis's arrest for murder and Frank's arrest for smuggling. I'm afraid what might happen if you go out.'

I felt my pulse begin to race. 'Why?'

'The town is split over all this. Some say Dennis has always been a bad one and they're not surprised he killed Leroy. Some say Dennis would never have killed Leroy – they grew up together, and Dennis has never hurt a fly, despite all his bluster and shooting off shotguns when he's drunk and such. And some, I'm sorry, dear, blame you, and that FBI man who treated us so arrogantly.'

'Why on earth?'

'They say that if you two hadn't come nosing around Frank and Leroy wouldn't have gotten scared and Dennis wouldn't have killed Leroy.'

'I don't understand.'

'Anne told Constable Long that Leroy wanted out of the beef smuggling business because of all the government people snooping around here because of price controls. He was afraid they would get caught. So the FBI's figured that Dennis and Leroy argued and Dennis killed him so he could keep on with the smuggling business.'

'So the town either believes the FBI is wrong about Dennis, or they blame the government for Leroy's murder in the first place!'

'They're just human.'

'True.'

'More tea?'

'I would love some.'

Lenore took my mug into the kitchen.

Lily rose from the rug and came over to me, tail wagging, and put her paws and head on my knee.

'Come to comfort me, girl?' I asked, rubbing her head.

Her tail wagged so hard that it thumped the floor, and I realized I had half a cookie in my hand. Lenore was still in the kitchen, so I slipped the cookie to Lily, who was so deliriously happy that she dropped to the floor and rolled over so I could scratch her belly.

'Lily!' Lenore said, returning with my tea. 'Leave Louise alone!'

Lily ambled back to her rug by the stove and lay down on her rug, but she kept an eye fixed on me. We shared a secret, she and I. We'd been naughty.

'Then,' Lenore continued, 'you did find the body. Everyone will want to ask you about it.'

Of course. In a town like this a murder would be sensational. I knew I might testify at Dennis's trial and could not talk about the murder beforehand. I was right to stay away from all the townsfolk.

Except Anne. I had to clear up the birthday question for the Martin postcard file, just in case Lt. Collins reviewed it. If he noticed my error he would be bound to point it out to Egbert.

I would visit Anne after dinner. Then I could enjoy the

evening and tomorrow morning here in this cozy room with my book before I drove back to Washington.

Over our dinner of stew and crusty homemade bread, eaten at a scratched and stained kitchen table that I figured had been in Lenore's family for a couple of hundred years, I asked Lenore about Anne's state of mind. I wanted to be prepared for what I might find when I went to see her.

'She's doing all right,' Lenore said. 'She's always seemed real strong – emotionally, I mean. When she was just fifteen her grandmother died and she had to leave school. But she went to work at Bertie Woods' café and met Leroy there. And she put up with a lot of nonsense from people about her accent and being foreign and all. Of course, once she married Leroy she became an American.'

'She lived through the Boer War,' I said. 'Most of her family died. That would toughen anyone up, if it didn't destroy them.'

Lenore sliced another thick chunk from the loaf of hot bread for me. 'I reckon so. Do you know, I went with another woman from my church to sit with Anne for a while after Leroy's funeral, and we found her on her hands and knees, scrubbing Leroy's bloodstains out of the floor, calm as she could be!'

Solomons Island Road was nearly empty of traffic, which pleased me under the circumstances. I had pulled my hat low over my eyes and wrapped a scarf around my neck, and I was driving a car unfamiliar to the denizens of St Leonard, but still I feared being recognized. I didn't want anyone but Lenore and Anne to know I was here. I could count on their silence, I believed.

I found myself at the turn-off to the Martin house and drove carefully over the rough road, crossing the rickety bridge at Perrin Branch, now free of ice and flowing sluggishly. It was about a mile from the bridge to Anne's quaint cottage on the Chesapeake Bay, but it might as well be fifty, it was so isolated.

I slammed on my brakes, forewarned by instinct before I

actually registered the deer that leapt across the road in front of me. I felt a bump, but the deer – scrawny and small, it must have been starving in this cold winter – continued leaping, vanishing into the woods to the left of the road. My madly pumping heart slowed, and I got out of the car with my torch. Please don't let Phoebe's car be damaged, I prayed. I could afford to fix it, but I didn't want her to think I was an unreliable driver. She might not let me borrow the car again.

I couldn't find even a mark on the car. Thank goodness.

Then I heard it. Music. I could swear I heard music.

The wind was blowing from the bay. Could it be coming from Anne's house? I doused my torch and listened, bending into the wind. It was music, all right, orchestral music. It must be quite loud for me to be able to hear it. How odd.

Listen to your gut, my instructors at the Farm told me over and over again. Don't be sanguine about anything.

I got back into the car and maneuvered it into the sheltered spot in the woods across from Anne's cottage that Williams and I had discovered on our stakeout.

When I got out of the car I listened for the music again. Not a sound, except for one optimistic bird song. I felt foolish. So what if Anne was listening to her record player?

But the music had seemed so loud, and, frankly, it sounded German. No one these days played anything by German composers. Stupid, really, what did Bach or Beethoven have to do with the war, but still it made people feel patriotic to eschew all things German.

I cautiously made my way through the copse. I didn't want to fall or switch on my flashlight. When I got to the edge of the woods I saw Anne's house. It was completely blacked out. The wind changed, and I could hear music again. I'm not an expert on German composers, but it sure wasn't Aaron Copland. I hesitated, still feeling ridiculous; what did it matter if Anne was listening to Bach?

To my left was the head of the Martins' inlet. I didn't see the mast of the skipjack at the pier. That was odd.

I found the path that led along the bank of the inlet to the head of the pier. A long black low-lying vessel was tied up there, floating gently, silhouetted against what little light there was.

It was a submarine.

TEN

I ducked behind a tree, propping myself up against its rough trunk to support legs that threatened to collapse under me.

Like Saul when he received the Holy Ghost, the scales fell from my eyes. The postcard from Richard Martin in Nantes *did* refer to a Nazi covert operation. Named 'Mother'. That would commence around February thirteenth, Anne's 'birthday'.

This sub was German. Had to be. Why would an American submarine be hidden in an oysterman's cove in Maryland?

Why was I so shocked? This had happened before.

On May twenty-eighth, 1942, last summer, a team of Nazi saboteurs left the submarine base in St Lorient, France on *U-202* bound for the South Shore of Long Island, near East Hampton.

The team was led by George John Dasch. Dasch had served in the German army during World War One, then emigrated to America, where he had worked as a waiter. When war broke out in September 1939, he impulsively went home, where he was recruited as a saboteur because of his fluent English and American mannerisms.

Dasch's four-man team was assigned to destroy the hydroelectric plants at Niagara Falls, the Aluminum Company of America factories in Illinois, Tennessee and New York, as well as the Philadelphia Salt Company's cryolite plant in Philadelphia, which supplied raw material for aluminum manufacture. They were also instructed to bomb locks on the Ohio River between Louisville, Ky., and Pittsburgh, Pa.

The four saboteurs in Dasch's team carried thousands of dollars for living expenses, bribes and travel. They were supplied with four waterproof wooden crates, each about twice the size of a shoebox. Three were filled with dynamite, some pieces disguised as lumps of coal. The fourth box carried fuses, timing devices, wire, incendiary pen and pencil sets and sulfuric acid.

U-202 made the 3,000-mile-plus trip across the Atlantic in fifteen days, traveling underwater during the day, on the surface at night. At eight o'clock Friday evening, June twelfth, *U-202* came within sight of the American coast. She submerged and slowly crept closer, grounding about fifty yards off the shore at eleven p.m. Because of the fog, visibility was terrible.

Dressed as German marines – so they would not be shot as spies if they were caught during the landing – Dasch and his team crawled into an inflatable rubber boat, and their crates were loaded aboard. Two armed German sailors rowed the boat to shore, where the sabotage team changed into civilian clothing.

While the others were burying the crates and uniforms, Dasch climbed over a dune to reconnoiter. Unexpectedly, he spotted a young Coast Guardsman heading toward him, waving a flashlight. Terrified that the Coast Guardsman would spot the half-buried boxes and the rest of his team, Dasch quickly walked to meet him.

Dasch told the Coast Guardsman that he and some friends on the beach were stranded fishermen. The Coast Guardsman suggested they take shelter at the Coast Guard station, less than half a mile away. Dasch declined, saying that he and his friends had no IDs or fishing permits. Not surprisingly, the young Coast Guardsman became suspicious.

Dasch offered the Coast Guardsman a bribe, which he pretended to accept. But Seaman 2nd Class John Cullen ran back to the Coast Guard station and roused his colleagues. They picked up weapons and hurried back to the beach. Dasch and the others were gone. But through the fog, the Coast Guardsmen spotted the departing submarine. When they searched the beach, they found freshly dug holes and, inside of them, the four wooden munitions crates, as well as a duffel bag filled with German uniforms.

The saboteurs might never have been found, but George Dasch, who regretted leaving America for Germany, had always intended to betray the operation as soon as the team arrived in the United States.

By midmorning he'd arrived in Washington, checked into the Mayflower Hotel and called the FBI.

Who knew what Dasch's team might have accomplished had Dasch not betrayed them? Since then the Coast Guard and the Navy had kept close watch over Atlantic beaches.

But the Chesapeake Bay was supposed to be impregnable to Nazi submarines!

I didn't know if Leroy was involved in this scheme, or what his murder might have to do with it, but clearly Anne was central to the story, a Nazi agent. Anne, so lovely, so stoic, so happy to be an American!

What did I do now? I reviewed my training from the Farm. Hide, reconnoiter, verify and communicate.

Even if half the submarine crew came out of Anne's house, where I was sure they were holed up, listening to Bach and drinking, they couldn't see me. I was concealed in the woods, under the low branches of a cedar tree, on the other side of the driveway from Anne's cottage. The moon was a mere sliver in the sky when it could be seen through the clouds and fog of the Chesapeake Bay.

What about Phoebe's car? I glanced at the house to make sure the blackout shades were still drawn and no one was outside on the porch, then slipped back to its hiding place. It was well concealed down the sandy track into the tiny clearing in the woods that Williams and I had discovered.

Broken tree branches felled by the weight of ice littered the woods. I collected some of the thickest branches I could find and piled them around Phoebe's car, camouflaging it from even a nearby observer.

Poor Phoebe! What would she think if she knew!

I crept back to my hiding place under the tree across from Anne's cottage when I heard a door slam. Music leaked out into the night, and with it the low hum of conversation in another language. Ever so carefully I edged around the tree truck. A man stood outside Anne's front door, silhouetted by the light of the half-open door behind him. He struck a match, and its flare revealed the peaked white cap and long black leather greatcoat of a captain in the Kriegsmarine. The captain cupped his hands around the cigarette and inhaled until it was well lit. The orange glow floated in the dark. While he puffed on his cigarette, the captain surveyed his surroundings, almost clinically, starting from the Martins' shed, proceeding past the driveway until he stared directly at my hiding place.

I'd already slumped until I was almost lying on the ground, sweating in the cold night air. I knew beyond all doubt now. This was a German sub, complete with captain and crew. How had it gotten past the forts, the searchlights, the contact mines, the submarine nets at the mouth of the Chesapeake Bay? Even more critical, what was its mission?

The captain crushed his cigarette under his boot and went back inside the cottage, where I expected Anne had prepared food and drink for him and his crew. It might be crowded inside the little house, but it would feel like a ballroom compared to the interior of the submarine after a two-week trip across the Atlantic. On board the sub the crew shared one toilet and one sink. Their sleeping hammocks, shared by two seamen on different shifts, would be filthy. Fresh foods supplies were either spent or spoiled. And after their mission was concluded, there was another two-week trip back across the Atlantic to look forward to.

Time to reconnoiter and verify.

I kept my unlit flashlight in my hand, for use as a weapon as much as any other function, and crept down to the dock. I wished I hadn't worn shoes with heels and a suit! I'd wanted to look professional for my visit to Prince Frederick. Why hadn't I changed into trousers and saddle shoes!

The submarine was draped in camouflage netting, but up close the netting didn't hide any of its features. I didn't know a lot about submarines, but I could tell this was a small one, not one of the newest denizens of the Nazi Wolf Pack. I paced off its length – one hundred and thirty feet. Its draught would be about twelve feet, easily fitting up against the tire-cushioned dock in the deep inlet. The conning tower, which contained the periscope, rose over my head. A snorkel, which allowed the diesel engine to power the sub and recharge its batteries while cruising just under the surface of the water, nestled next to it. An antiaircraft gun was mounted next to the conning tower.

I figured that because of its size the sub's crew couldn't number more than twenty-five, squeezed into every nook and cranny of the vessel. How many torpedoes could it carry? Five at the most? And I doubted this ship contained enough fuel to do more than get it here and back across the Atlantic to France.

This was a vessel designed to patrol the European Coast before the United States entered the war, commandeered for this operation because of its small size.

The submarine drifted up against the dock, so close to me that I could reach out and touch it. It was coated in rubber! We'd heard rumors at OSS that the Nazis were testing rubber shields to absorb sonar waves, and here was proof. Camouflage nets weren't standard equipment for subs either.

A gust of wind blew aside the curtain of fog so I could scout the length of the inlet for Leroy's skipjack. It wasn't there. What a perfect transport for a team of spies! What could be more ordinary than a crew of oystermen sailing on the Chesapeake Bay? How many men would fit on a skipjack? Four? Six?

That left fewer than twenty men to sail the submarine back to France. Twenty Nazi seamen now packed into Anne's cottage.

I didn't bother to search for Nazi markings on the sub. The rubber probably concealed them, and I'd been on the dock too long already, at least five minutes. The submarine captain had to be very complacent not to post a guard on the dock. But then no one could possibly see the sub from the Bay, and the only way to get to the house was two miles down the Martins' driveway.

I scuttled back to my hiding place under the tree at the head of the inlet to think. Briefly, because I had to take some kind of action soon.

The tide had begun to ebb. I reasoned that the sub had arrived with the last high tide and the captain had immediately dispatched the saboteurs on Leroy's skipjack. The crew would rest at Anne's cottage until high tide early tomorrow morning, when they would leave. It would still be dark, and they couldn't stay docked at the Martin inlet during daylight. Despite the isolation of Anne's cottage, tomorrow anyone could come by Anne's to visit, like Lenore and her friend had after Leroy's funeral.

*   *   *

I checked my watch. Another five minutes had passed.

Now it was time to call the cavalry, but that wasn't as simple as it seemed. I could drive to Lenore's house and use her telephone. But whom would I call? At night in the entire county there was only one policeman on duty. If he was out of his office answering a summons I couldn't reach him. Even if I did, would he believe me?

I couldn't call the Solomons Island naval training station or the Patuxent River Air Station because all military phone numbers were unlisted! I could try phoning Washington, either my office at OSS or the FBI, but I didn't expect whoever was manning the switchboard to believe me, and it could take hours for my news to travel up the chain of command to someone who could call out the troops.

And somewhere on the waters of the Chesapeake Bay was a team of Nazi saboteurs on a deadly mission, with dozens of targets to choose from! They could sail that skipjack up to Annapolis or Baltimore or down to Norfolk and catch a bus or a train to anywhere in the country. They would possess perfect IDs, authentic accents and plenty of money.

I heard the door of the cottage slam again. I glanced around the tree trunk and saw two German seamen, wearing grey leather jackets, trousers, and brimless black caps, leave Anne's cottage, rifles slung over their shoulders, and move down the driveway toward the main road.

No, no! I'd waited too late to drive away! What if the guards were posted between Phoebe's car and the highway?

I had no choice but to find out.

I would give anything to be wearing practical shoes. And trousers! Instead I was navigating the woods, oyster-shell paths, and pockets of sand in pumps, stockings, and my good wool coat. At least it wasn't as cold as it had been last week.

I paused at the edge of the woods, peering out into the night. My eyes ached from the strain, but I saw nothing moving. How close would the seamen dare venture to the main road? I crept down the road, almost a mile, to the bridge over the creek, and then I saw them. They were standing on my side of the bridge smoking cigarettes, the idiots. I could see the glow in the deep darkness. If they weren't smoking I might have walked right into them.

I trekked back to my hiding place under the tree facing Anne's cottage, feeling desperate. And tired. I'd hiked two miles to discover that I was trapped between the guards on the road and the Chesapeake Bay, with no way to communicate with the Coast Guard or the Navy.

The moon peered through the clouds again, and below it blazed the light at the Cove Point lighthouse, its beam stabbing into the dark sky out to sea.

That was it!

The lighthouse at Cove Point stood on a bluff above the beach less than two miles south from here. In fact, the Nazi captain had probably used its beacon to find the Martins' inlet. The Coast Guardsmen on duty would be able to radio their headquarters! This had to be the fastest way to call for help.

I'd need to slip down to the beach and make my way south along the coast, in the dark and cold, for two miles or so, but how else could I sound the alarm?

I needed to move now, before some Nazi wandered out onto the cottage porch or down to the dock to check on the sub! As before, I used the cover of the woods to shelter me until I reached the head of the dock. Then I dropped to my hands and knees and crawled down its length, passing the submarine on my way and collecting splinters in my knees. When I got to the middle of the dock, where it left the land and began to stretch out into the Bay, I jumped onto the cold sand of the beach. It was a rough landing; the dock was higher off the beach than I realized, and my glasses flew off. I spent a few nerve-racking minutes rooting around in the sand looking for them, then found them, thank goodness, or I would have been helpless, and took off running south.

These goddamned shoes! Frustrated by my progress, I kicked off my pumps and ran barefoot along the beach, truly barefoot, as within seconds my stockings were shredded away from my feet. It was a brand new pair, too. Soon my coat, my new coat with the fur collar I so loved, was soaked with sea spray until it was unbearably heavy, and I flung it off, powered by the image of a half dozen Nazi agents dispersing around the country.

It was slow going. Despite running barefoot along the edge of the Bay, my feet sank into the sand. Once I stepped on a pile of oyster shells, slicing into my feet. I ran wildly, since no one could see me, desperate to make progress. Occasionally, the fog horn sounded, or I caught sight of the lighthouse beam, and I could see wooden steps leading up from the beach to shuttered summer cottages, dinghies overturned at the edge of the dunes, or a crab pot that had ripped loose from its buoy.

I figured I was halfway there, my eyes fixed ahead on the lighthouse lantern, when my feet tripped over rock, and I fell forward onto a wide stone ledge, twisting an ankle and landing on my left arm. God, please don't let anything be broken! I sat up and allowed myself to flick on my flashlight. I'd fallen right onto a rough rock jetty that protruded eighteen inches above the sand. I was lucky I hadn't cracked my head open. My ankle and arm hurt like crazy, but after massaging them both it seemed nothing was broken. My feet dripped blood from the oyster shells. The cold sand must have numbed them because I felt no pain.

With my flashlight trained at my feet I picked my way across the jetty and hit the beach again. I ran with a limp, but run I did, my eyes fixed on the light from the lighthouse lantern, until I could see the lighthouse and the Coast Guard station next to it above me on a bluff.

I quailed at the sight of the three flights of wooden staircase that led from the beach to the lighthouse. But I grabbed both rails and pulled myself up as much as climbed the stairs. When I reached the flat top of the bluff I flung myself onto the grass. The lighthouse and its outbuildings were just steps away from me, but I couldn't get there until I'd caught my breath.

The lighthouse was squat and conical, stone painted white, with a black round lantern perched on top that housed the light. A small white hut nearby, with a latticed cubical on top of it, was labeled 'fog horn'. The outline of a shed or barn was visible behind it.

I staggered toward the keeper's house, a two-story clapboard building with a front porch stretching across the front of the building. A flagpole without a flag stood tall nearby. One downstairs room was lit.

I threw myself on the door of the house, pounding frantically. The door was opened by a Coast Guardsman holding a rifle in the low ready position.

'Who the hell are you?' he asked.

'My name is Louise Pearlie,' I said. Should I tell him I worked for OSS? Better not. He wouldn't believe me. 'I've seen Germans,' I said. 'In an inlet up the coast!'

'Lady, everyone thinks they've seen Germans.'

'There's a submarine!'

'Sure there is. Come inside, and keep your hands where I can see them,' he said, motioning me into the house with his rifle.

'You must believe me! There's a German sub in the Martins' inlet north of here! Covered with camouflage netting. The crew is inside the cottage!'

I guessed from the man's uniform that he was a Chief Petty Officer. He was not a young man. His short brown hair was flecked with grey, and deep creases divided his face. This man was a veteran who'd spent years on the water under the sun.

Those eyes narrowed, and he backed away from me, lifting his rifle slightly.

'I'm not crazy, I swear.' I didn't bother with the details of the OSS investigation or Leroy's murder; it would only make me less believable.

'I was in town and went to visit Anne Martin,' I said. 'Her husband just died. I saw the submarine in their inlet! And the captain outside on her porch lighting a cigarette!'

'You're a mess. You aren't wearing a coat. You're barefoot, and your legs and feet are bloody.'

'I took off my shoes so I could run on the beach, and I fell on the stone jetty. My coat got soaked with water so I threw it away. You've got to call the Solomons Island base! Who knows what the Germans are planning! Please!'

'Lady, my career would be over if I reported a Nazi submarine in the Bay and it wasn't true. Which I don't expect it is.'

I heard a clatter on the stairs. Another Coast Guardsman, pulling suspenders over his shirt, ran down the stairs, pulling up short when he saw me.

'Who is this?' he asked.

'Seaman, this woman claims to have seen a German submarine in the Bay. What do you think?'

'Not possible, sir. God himself couldn't get past the firepower at the mouth of the Bay.'

'I swear,' I said. Damn it, I'd left my purse in Phoebe's car, and I had no way at all to identify myself. 'You simply must believe me!'

The seaman looked down and saw my legs and feet, and his mouth dropped open. A small pool of blood had collected around my toes.

'What would happen to your career, Chief Petty Officer . . .' I began.

'Jarvis.'

'Jarvis, if there was a German submarine in the Bay and you knew about it and didn't report it?'

'I'd find myself patrolling Cold Bay in the Aleutians,' he said.

'So you'll call the base?'

'No, ma'am. I'm not that gullible. But it's just possible you're telling the truth, and I can't ignore it. I'm going to see your sub for myself.'

'That will take too long! And there are Nazi seamen guarding the Martins' driveway!'

'We'll go the way you came. And you're going with me. Seaman, find this woman some foul-weather gear while I saddle up Missy.'

I turned down the seaman's offer to bandage my feet. I wanted nothing to slow down our departure.

'I'm fine,' I said to him. 'These are just scratches.'

The seaman handed me an armful of gear and showed me to the bathroom. I tore my suit skirt from the hem to the waist, front and back, and stuffed the flaps into the rubber bib overalls I pulled on. The skirt was damp, but I needed some insulation between my legs and the overalls. Then I stretched heavy wool socks over my battered feet and shoved them deep into sea boots. An alpaca-lined parka hung down to my knees. I topped off this charming ensemble with a sou'wester, a waterproof hat with ear guards and a brim that covered my neck. I'd be well protected from cold and sea spray on my journey back to the inlet.

'Missy' was not the name I would have bestowed on Jarvis's horse. 'Big Bertha' would be more appropriate. The animal was huge. She had to be part draft horse. A pretty one, too: fuzzy, with a thick grey winter coat and white feathers of hair hanging over her hooves. Her tail arched and swished as she pranced. Was there such a program as Horses for Defense? Missy seemed more like a show horse than a military animal.

'We use her to patrol the beach,' Jarvis said. 'She never wears out.'

Jarvis turned to his seaman. 'Roust seaman Grady out of his bunk,' he said. 'Both of you need to be combat ready. If I'm not back in an hour call HQ and tell them what's happened. Then I want Grady to stay with the light and sound the fog horn. Remember the emergency warning interval?'

'Ten minutes,' the seaman said.

'Correct. And you come down to the beach and work your way north. Miss . . .' He looked at me. 'What is your name again?'

'Mrs Louise Pearlie.' There was something about 'Mrs' that seemed to earn respect from men. Using it came in handy sometimes.

'Mrs Pearlie and I might be needing your help. Ready?' he said to me.

I had never been on a horse before. Only adrenaline and my determination to get back to the Martins' cottage persuaded me to grasp the hand Jarvis stretched out to me. He hauled me up behind him, and I banged my knee on the rifle slung over his saddle.

I locked my arms around Jarvis as he gathered up the horse's reins. Missy danced with anticipation, her bridle jingling. I felt like one of those heroines on the cover of a pulp romance novel!

The only way I'd seen up from the beach to the bluff where

the lighthouse stood were the wooden stairs I'd scaled, but there was a hairpin path that led down the other side of the bluff to the beach. Missy went down it way too fast to suit me, but she'd clearly navigated it many times before and put her hooves down confidently. She leapt the last couple of feet to the beach, throwing me into Jarvis. He said something, but the wind blew it away and I couldn't understand him.

Missy thundered up the beach. At this pace we'd be at the foot of the Martins' dock in no time flat.

I'd forgotten the stone jetty. Jarvis hadn't; he slowed as we approached it, and then pulled Missy to a halt. He turned around to me.

'Missy can't cross this,' he said. 'She could injure herself badly. We'll have to go around it.'

I looked landward. A cliff rose off the beach to the top of the bluff. The wooden staircase that led up to a shuttered cottage had two full flights of steps. The horse couldn't possibly navigate such a steep cliff.

Before I'd finished my thought, Jarvis pulled Missy to the right. Without hesitation she plunged into the surf. I held on for dear life as a wave broke over us, sending salt spray and freezing water cascading down our bodies. Missy powered forward, her broad chest parting the waves. I could see her shoulders working and feel her hooves searching for purchase on the sea floor. Then we were beyond the surf and the horse was swimming. Swimming! Water flowed past us like a river. For once the sky above was clear and bright with stars and the light of a quarter moon.

The two of them, man and horse, must have done this before on beach patrol. Jarvis knew when the jetty ended out beyond the waves, and he turned the horse north again. She swam parallel to the beach for a minute or two, then Jarvis urged her back towards the beach. Now the waves battered us from behind, but I felt Missy's hooves catch the sand and soon we were on the beach again. The horse shook herself like a wet dog, almost throwing us off.

Thanks to my rubber overalls and parka I wasn't too wet, but I couldn't see out of my salt-encrusted glasses.

Jarvis didn't permit Missy to gallop again. Instead he kept

her to a walk while he peered ahead. The Cove Point light was behind and above us, but fog had moved in again and obscured our vision.

'I think this is a good place to leave Missy,' he said.

He lowered me to the ground, which felt hard and unyielding under my feet after the sensation of swimming on horseback. Jarvis slung his leg over the saddle and dropped to his feet himself, pulling Missy's reins over her head.

He led the horse up the beach and slid her bridle off her head. She had a halter on under the bridle. Jarvis took a coil of rope from his saddle and tied her to a tree at the edge of the beach. 'That's so she doesn't jingle,' he said. 'She gets so excited.'

'You be quiet,' he said to her. 'No whinnying. No prancing. I'll be right back.' He gave her a peppermint, and she crunched on it with her big yellow teeth as we moved away.

Jarvis and I crept along the beach until we saw the Martins' dock. I pulled him down behind a dune until we squatted on the beach next to the dock. Whispering directly into his ear, I briefed him about the area. I explained that the dock ran along the shoreline of the inlet before reaching out into the Bay. That a thick patch of woods stretched from the northern side of the Martins' driveway, where my car was hidden, most of the way to the head of the dock, and up the side of the inlet. That the Martins' cottage was on the other side of the driveway, quite out in the open, but visible to someone carefully hidden in the woods across from it. That the Nazi guards were a mile up the driveway standing guard on the other side of the bridge that crossed Perrin Branch. That I was sure I could get to my car, but not past the guards at the bridge.

Jarvis absorbed all this without comment, just nodding.

We left our hiding place and scrabbled along the sand until we got to the dock. Then we pulled ourselves up until we could see out onto it. The submarine was still there, rocking gently up against the tires that cushioned the dock.

We ducked down below the driftwood again.

'Jesus H. Christ!' Jarvis said, in a whisper. He looked at me with new respect. 'Explain to me how you came to find this again?'

It would take way too long to tell him the entire story and would serve no purpose.

'I met Anne recently. I came back here for the weekend and heard that her husband had died, so I thought I'd drive over to express my sympathy. I parked my car up the road in the woods to protect my tires and walked down the driveway, and then I saw the submarine. I ducked right back into the woods.' So lucky no one had seen me!

'Why did you park your car in the woods? Who are you?'

'Nobody. I mean, I'm just a government girl. I'm a file clerk. I didn't want to drive the car over all those oyster shells. The car doesn't belong to me. I borrowed it from my landlady. What I don't understand is how the submarine got up here from the mouth of the Bay.'

'Just between you and me,' Jarvis whispered, 'it's possible. Because of the deep freeze.'

'What do you mean?'

'Eastern Command left the minefields in safe mode and the submarine nets open. Our own ships were crashing around in the ice and wind and in danger of hitting the mines.'

'You're kidding!'

'That's not all. Power outages disrupted the searchlights and the sonar. I expect your Nazi captain didn't plan to come up the Bay at all, but saw his chance and made a dash for it.'

Still crouched low, we scouted the dock, the cottage, and the lawn that ran from it down to the beach. There was no sound at all from the cottage, no light leaking around the blackout curtains.

'They must be asleep,' I said.

'I guarantee you there are still guards up the road,' Jarvis said.

Out of the corner of my eye something white moved, and I turned to look across the inlet from the submarine. It was the skipjack, tied up to a tree! I grabbed Jarvis's arm.

'What is it?' he said.

'The Martins' skipjack! It wasn't here earlier! I think I must have been right!'

'About what?' he whispered.

'That submarine is too small for combat duty,' I said. 'It

would barely have enough fuel to get across the Atlantic and back.'

'I was thinking the same thing.'

'Do you think it brought a team of saboteurs? Say they docked here during the last high tide, the team took off in the skipjack with one of the sailors from the submarine, got dropped off, and the sailor brought it back?'

'Jesus H. Christ,' he said again. 'I've got to get back to the lighthouse to call HQ. I expect the Germans will leave on the next high tide.'

It was already coming in.

'I need you to stay here,' he said to me. 'Keep watch. Do you still have a flashlight for signaling? Know Morse Code?'

'Yes,' I answered, to both questions.

'You *are* a spy,' he said.

For a second I was taken aback, but then I realized he was joking.

'Here,' Jarvis said, handing me his sidearm, the standard Colt .45 issued to most American servicemen. 'Can you use this? Of course you can, why am I even asking?'

I hefted the gun in my hand. It was good to have for self-defense, but I couldn't stop a submarine with it. In fact there was no way I could prevent the submarine from leaving the inlet if the cavalry didn't arrive in time. But of course it would. High tide was a couple of hours away yet. The Solomons Island naval training station was just a few miles down the road.

Jarvis turned to me. 'You do realize, don't you, that this woman, Anne, will leave with the Germans if she can?'

Of course she would, the traitor. I could not imagine why she had done what she did. How could she betray her adopted country, the one that offered her safety and security after she immigrated? And how did her treachery relate to the postcard from Leroy's 'cousin' in France?

It must have been meant for her, not Leroy, and signaled to her, what? And I had given her the postcard! She would need a suitcase radio to communicate, but Williams and I hadn't found one when we searched the house. But then Leroy's criminal adventure and murder distracted us from the postcard, and Anne, and her Nazi contact, must have decided to go ahead with the operation.

Jarvis slipped away to mount Missy and gallop back to the lighthouse.

I couldn't keep watch effectively if I froze to death or lost consciousness from pain. Now that I wasn't flush with adrenaline I began to shiver uncontrollably.

And worse, my feet began to register pain from the torture they'd endured from the sharp oyster shells and the stone jetty. They ached and throbbed relentlessly.

I needed to get warm. On the back seat of Phoebe's car was the blanket that was always kept there and the sweater I'd bought at the Frederick Courthouse. My purse too, which contained a bottle of aspirin. I needed to get to that car.

To do that I must to crawl up the dock again and slip into the woods at the head of the Martins' dock and make my way to the vehicle's hiding place. And hope that the Nazi submariners who were guarding the Martins' driveway stayed far down the road. They couldn't have found the car or the crew wouldn't have been sleeping peacefully in the cottage right now.

Again I crawled on my stomach up the dock, my head raised just enough to see where I was going. At least the rubber trousers I was wearing protected me from more splinters. At last I reached the woods, raised myself to a crouch and moved as quietly and quickly as I could.

It seemed like an age, but finally I got to the car. I moved a branch to crawl into the front seat. After the door closed I felt such relief at being out of the wind and off my feet that I allowed myself to cry, but only for a few minutes. I didn't have time for any more tears than that.

I maneuvered into the back seat of the car and stripped off my foul-weather gear and what was left of my suit and stockings. I buttoned my new thick warm blueberry sweater around me. Then I ripped Phoebe's blanket in half and wrapped one of the halves around my waist down to the top of my thighs, securing it with the belt from my skirt.

I couldn't delay dealing with my feet any longer. I pulled

off the sea boots. The wool socks Seaman Grady had given me had adhered to my feet and lower legs with dried blood. I peeled them off. It didn't hurt much, just started the bleeding again. I used more strips of blanket to wrap my feet and legs, securing them with safety pins from my handbag. I redressed in my foul-weather gear. At last I swallowed three aspirin, dry.

I really wished I had a martini. Instead I took one of the NoDoz Williams had given me so I wouldn't fall asleep.

An hour later the cavalry hadn't arrived, and I understood why. Finding the team of saboteurs was more important than capturing the Nazi submarine. Within minutes of Jarvis calling his HQ a manhunt would be on, involving the FBI, countless police forces, the Coast Guard and the military. They wouldn't have much time before the saboteurs would vanish. I had to wonder if any military assets at all would be deployed to capture the submarine. No one on board would know the saboteurs' missions, not even the Captain. And did the United States really want to detain a Nazi submarine in the Chesapeake Bay? What if word got out to the public that a submarine had made it past all the defenses at the mouth of the Bay? The morale consequences to the entire country would be devastating. Wouldn't it make strategic sense to allow the submarine to escape?

It made sense, but I was disgusted. In fact, I could hardly bear it. Especially if Anne escaped too. I wanted to see that woman behind bars or hanging from a gallows.

High tide was almost here. Time to take my station and keep watch, see if I could figure out the sub's bearing. There was just one hope to take out the submarine. If it could be tracked out into the Atlantic it could be captured or destroyed without fear of alerting the American public. But now that the weather had changed, surely the sub couldn't make it through the mouth of the Bay? Eastern Command couldn't count on all the soldiers and sailors on duty at Hampton Roads to allow a Nazi sub to escape and then keep such a secret.

Another option for the submarine was to cross the Bay, ditch the sub in another sheltered spot, and swim to the eastern shore. The Nazis could easily cross the rural peninsula and be picked up on the Atlantic shore by another sub. The more I thought about this, the more it seemed the obvious choice. Landing on the eastern shore might have been the sub's plan in the beginning, until the captain saw his chance during the artic cold snap to dash into the Bay itself.

I crouched down in my spot under the tree. Light shone around the edges of the cottage's blackout blinds. In the shadows on the porch I saw several men, indistinguishable from each other in their grey leathers and black caps, eating sandwiches and drinking from steaming mugs. A couple of crates sat on the porch. Fresh supplies for the long sea trip back to Germany? Supplies that Anne had gathered for them? More figures came out onto the porch. I saw the lights go out in the cottage. I felt sick. Small waves lapped high on the shore of the inlet. They'd be leaving soon.

I squinted, hoping to pick out Anne in the mass of seamen collecting on the front porch of the cottage and in the yard. Soon it seemed at least twenty were milling around. I noticed a slight figure wearing loose leathers and with what looked like hair up in a bun. It had to be Anne. She, because I was sure it was her, carried a small bag, just a little bigger than a handbag, that was feminine, not a sailor's sea bag. She'd probably taken no more than a change of underwear, the picture of her family, and her pearls. There wouldn't be room for more in the submarine. A woman crammed into the cramped submarine with all those men would have a most unpleasant journey. But she'd been through worse, hadn't she?

The Captain walked out onto the porch, commanding in his black leathers and peaked cap, and all the men, and the one woman, came to attention. He barked out his orders, and the crew moved quickly toward the inlet, the dock, and the submarine.

As I watched the crew prepare the submarine for departure, I thought about Jarvis's gun. It had eight bullets. I could do some damage with eight bullets before they could stop me. But not to Anne. She was the first 'crewman' who'd descended into the submarine. Now there were just two seamen on the dock untying the ropes that held it there. Another two, including the captain, stood on the conning tower scanning the area with binoculars.

I groped around the deep pocket in my oilskin and grasped Jarvis's gun, fully understanding the expression 'itchy trigger finger'. There was nothing I could do with the gun, but I felt better holding it, imagining myself shooting someone, anyone, the captain, or Anne. Even running down the dock and pumping every bullet into the hull of the sub appealed to me. The bullets would ricochet off the steel plate and kill me, of course, but that didn't stop me from relishing the prospect.

The submarine slowly moved out of the Martins' inlet with the high tide. Once clear of the inlet I saw it turn toward the Bay. The sub would cruise on the surface of the water as long as possible while the diesel engine charged its batteries, only submerging if its sonar picked up a vessel nearby. Since it was Sunday, and as foggy as the Chesapeake Bay can be on an early winter morning, traffic on the Bay would be light.

I watched until I could barely see the submarine, then crawled down the dock for the last time. The submarine could change its bearing anytime, but to me it appeared to be heading due east. I could see in my mind's eye, as if it was actually happening, the sub cruising into one of the deep coves on the eastern shore of Maryland. The crew would abandon ship, scuttle the sub, and hide in the woods that edged the shore. When night fell they'd split into small groups, make their way across the quiet farms and pastures of the eastern shore, and meet again at some predetermined spot on the Atlantic coast. There rubber dinghies from another German submarine, a big new one, would ferry them out to the sub and they would head back to one of the impregnable submarine bases on the coast of France. Anne would escape too. I could picture some SS officer pinning an Iron Cross on her chest!

I understood Eastern Command's decision not to detain the submarine. I did, really, but I hated it with every fiber of my being.

I got to my sore feet and lingered at the end of the dock, looking toward the spot where I'd last seen the submarine, Jarvis's Colt .45 dangling at my side.

*   *   *

It was time to do something about my own disordered condition. Get back to Lenore's and clean myself up. I hoped I could get upstairs without her seeing me. I would need to call Williams and make myself available to the FBI for debriefing. And I'd make a verbal report to Lawrence Egbert at OSS first thing in the morning and then write a written report for, what else, the files! It made me queasy to think of General Donovan or even the President reading it, but that was inevitable. I would tell no lies. I'd realized the French postcard file was incomplete, even though we'd closed the investigation, and perfectionist that I was I decided to verify Anne's birthday while on a holiday weekend trip. I found a German submarine docked at her cottage and notified the Coast Guard as soon as possible. End of report. Signed Mrs Louise Pearlie, OSS Registry Research Assistant.

But the Martins' cottage, so quaint and picturesque in its clearing, beckoned to me. The FBI would be crawling all over it in a couple of hours, after Eastern Command was sure the submarine was out of the Bay, looking for clues to the targets of the saboteurs. FBI photographers would snap pictures of every square inch of the place but I'd earned the right to see it for myself first.

The door to the cottage wasn't locked. It swung open, and I went inside. Clearly, twenty men had spent twelve hours here. The floor under my feet in the entry was caked with dirt and mud. In the once tidy kitchen, plates, glasses, and cups were stacked on every surface. Greasy pots and pans were piled in the stone sink. Toast crumbs and coffee grounds crunched under my feet. A half-empty milk bottle rested on a window sill, and I had to edge around a crate of empty beer bottles to get to the sitting room, where blankets and pillows were strewn all over the floor, sofa and chairs.

The bathtub looked as if all twenty of the Nazi seamen had bathed and washed out their allotted two pairs of underwear in it.

It seemed the seamen had stayed out of the bedroom and that Anne had slept alone. The bed was unmade but not tossed, one of the drawers in the dresser was ajar, and the picture of her family and her pearls were indeed missing. Other than that the room was orderly.

I was done here for good. It was time for me to go.

ELEVEN

Anne sat in Leroy's desk chair with her legs crossed as if she was at a tea party. I started as if I'd seen a ghost. 'What, no questions for me?' she asked. 'No interrogation about postcards and such?'

'Where did you come from?' I asked.

'The shed. I was waiting there to see if you'd come out of the woods. It took you long enough. I got cold, and I wanted a cigarette.'

Anne had altered her appearance significantly. If I'd caught sight of her somewhere else I don't know if I'd have recognized her. She'd dyed her hair a deep brown and twisted it into a bun at the nape of her head. Perched on her head was a stylish grey fedora that matched a wool coat thrown over the arm of her chair. She wore a smart dove-grey flannel suit and pumps that matched her roomy black pocketbook. Thick make-up – eyeshadow, rouge, and lipstick – coated her face.

'Where was the radio?' I asked. She must have had a suitcase radio.

'Hidden in the skipjack under the canvas,' she said. The one place Williams and I hadn't searched. 'It has new owners now.'

Anne must have handed over the radio to the team of spies and saboteurs the submarine had brought. What an efficient use of assets.

I would have happily lunged at her then, but couldn't because she pulled a Luger out of her handbag and trained it on me. She motioned me over to her, stood up, and patted me down, finding the Colt and my knife in the pockets of my coat. She tucked them into her large handbag.

'Sit down next to me,' she said, sitting on the sofa and patting the cushion next to her. 'You must be tired. You look like you washed up on the beach from a shipwreck.'

I perched on the arm of the sofa instead. 'You expected me,' I said. 'How did you know I was here?'

'Lenore called last night about midnight. She said she was worried that you hadn't come home from visiting me. I told her you'd fallen asleep on the sofa and I didn't want to wake you up. Oh, and we're spending the day together. You're going to help me clean out Leroy's things and take them to a thrift shop in Washington for me.'

'Richard Martin's postcard was your signal that the submarine was on its way, wasn't it?'

'So many questions,' she said. 'What a curious young woman you are. But we don't have time to go into all that right now.'

'I expected you to leave with the Germans,' I said.

She made a disgusted face. 'Live in Germany? That awful place! What a nauseating culture the Nazis have created. I'm not a Nazi!'

'You're doing a damn good imitation of one. Are you going to kill me?'

'Not if you do exactly as I say. It's so convenient that you have a car. Let's find you some clothes, though, before we leave. You'd attract the attention of a blind man looking the way you do.'

'Good lord,' she said, as I stripped down to my underwear in her bedroom. 'You're creative, I give you that.'

Anne was a bit heavier and taller than me, but with the help of a belt notched in its last hole I gathered a pair of her wool trousers around my waist. When she saw my feet she grimaced, but I just shrugged and pulled on a pair of Leroy's heavy socks. I added a flannel shirt, buttoned my new blueberry sweater over it, and pulled on my sea boots again.

On our way out of the front door Anne found me a pea coat to replace the Navy-issued parka Jarvis had given me. I was warm for the first time in hours.

'Here.' She handed me a wicker basket waiting by the door. 'Sandwiches and coffee,' she said, as if we were going on a picnic. 'We won't want to stop anywhere public to eat.'

She urged me down the path to the shed and nudged the door open with her foot. 'Get one of the cans of gas,' she said.

It was heavy, and I struggled back up the path ahead of her with both the basket and the gas can, her Lugar just inches from my back.

This wasn't going to end well for me. Once we got out into the country Anne could put a bullet in my head and dump my remains into some stream or river. She'd had more rest and food than I had and no injuries. She'd have Phoebe's car. She could escape as cleanly as if she'd left on the submarine.

'Wait a minute,' Anne said. Keeping the Luger trained on me she edged over to the dock, drew Jarvis's Colt from her bag and threw it into the water.

When we got to the car, Anne gave it the once-over. 'This will do,' she said. 'Fill the gas tank.'

I did, and she flung the empty can into the woods. When I opened the car trunk to stow the basket she noticed the gas can I'd brought from Phoebe's.

'Any left in that one?' she asked.

'Almost full,' I said.

'Good,' she said. 'Let's get out of here.'

'Where are we going?' I asked.

'You don't need to know that right now,' she said. She sat in the passenger seat next to me with the Luger cradled in her lap. 'Just turn right on St Leonard Road.'

North. If we stayed on Solomons Island Road we could be in Annapolis, or even Baltimore, by tonight.

We cruised through St Leonard, shut down tight on this Sunday morning, past the Esso station and Bertie Woods' café.

The first floor of Lenore's guesthouse was bright with light. I imagined Lenore baking bread or muffins, with Lily at her feet hoping for a bite.

'If you're not going to kill me, why take me along with you?' I asked.

'I need someone to tell my story when this is all over.'

'So what *is* your story? You told me you were proud to be an American, that you were happy here.'

'Oh, I am, and I was. I'm going to start a new life somewhere else in the United States. The Nazis provided me with documents.'

'That makes no sense. You must be insane!'

'Not at all. I just hate the British more than I love the United States.'

I shifted gears as I braked at the stoplight on Courthouse Square in Prince Frederick. 'You did this because you hate the British? How does that work?'

'If the Allies lose, Hitler will rule Great Britain. What a glorious, splendid thought!'

'Why!'

'The British destroyed my life. During the Boer War.'

'That seems farfetched to me.'

'Farfetched,' she said, taking her eyes off the road and turning to me. Her eyes burned into mine. 'Farfetched! The British army burned our farmhouse to the ground. They salted our fields and butchered our livestock, even our pets. My father and older brother died fighting in the war. My mother and younger brother died of typhoid fever in Bloemfontein concentration camp. We'd been a wealthy family, but when my grandmother and I arrived here we shared one room at a boarding house. She worked as a seamstress to support us.'

'It's terrible what happened to you and your family,' I said. 'But think what this war is doing to innocent American families. You've set Nazis loose in our country!'

She shrugged. 'War is ugly,' she said. 'People die. Are you hungry? You must be. There's a lane coming up we can turn down.'

I drove about a mile down a dirt road canopied with bare oak trees and shielded from the main road with chokeberry bushes. The lane ended at a rusty metal gate that hadn't been opened in years.

We had our picnic – there was no other good word for it – in the car. I hadn't eaten since dinner yesterday. Anne had made ham and cheese sandwiches with plenty of mayonnaise and homemade bread, leftovers from the feast she'd prepared for her German guests. The sandwiches were delicious. With a cup of coffee and food my dizziness disappeared, but I was exhausted.

'You look all done in,' Anne said to me. 'I was up all night too. We'll nap here until dusk.'

Anne tied my hands to the steering wheel with a length of rope she'd packed into the picnic basket. Did she really think I could sleep here?

I woke up with my head resting on the steering wheel.

Anne was awake and already outside, opening my door, untying my wrists, and gesturing me over to a bush to take care of my business, her Luger in her hand.

'Hurry up,' she said, 'and we'll be on our way. We've slept all afternoon.'

Twenty miles later we turned east on Maryland State Road Four, towards Washington. Inside the city it became Pennsylvania Avenue.

'Turn north on Second Street,' Anne said.

Union Station! That must be Anne's plan. If she didn't intend to kill me, she could tie my hands to the wheel again and leave me in Phoebe's car in a deserted alley. I wouldn't be found until morning, and by then she'd be long gone, her destination unknown. That sounded like a good plan to me, and I clung to it.

Instead we turned on Massachusetts.

'Please tell me where we are going,' I asked. My nerves were taut, and I wondered what she planned to do with me. The more time I spent with her, the more unbalanced I thought she was.

'You'll see.' Anne seemed edgy, even excited. She gripped her handbag as if it held a sack of gold coins.

We passed the Post Office and the Government Printing Office. Six blocks later we reached Mt. Vernon Square, where the Washington Public Library, with its stunning marble façade, sat regally, ruling over the entire square. When I first lived in DC I'd spent many Saturdays reading magazines and newspapers from all over the world in the War Reading Room.

'Go around to the back of the library,' Anne said. 'There's a staff parking lot down a ramp, on the lower level. Park the car there.'

I did as I was told. The lot was empty except for our car.

'What are we doing here?'

'Waiting until it's good and dark,' she said.

For what, I wondered. Why was she delaying her escape? It was still possible that Eastern Command would capture those Nazi submariners on the eastern shore of Maryland and learn she wasn't with them. And I dearly hoped someone was missing me enough to do something about it.

'I took a course here when I started working at the St Leonard Library,' Anne mused. 'The Town Council paid for it. It was the best week of my life. I stayed at a boarding house a couple of blocks away and walked here every day for classes. I didn't cook a single meal. Look,' she said, rummaging around in her purse, 'I kept the key to the staff entrance.'

So, she was going to kill me and dump my body in the library, where my corpse wouldn't be found until tomorrow morning.

She caught my frightened expression.

'Don't look so stricken. This is the perfect place for me to lock you up until I'm out of the city and for me to wait for a bus where no one can see me.'

Anne seemed almost feverish as she grabbed something in her purse and held on to it so I couldn't see it.

'Guess what this is,' she said.

'I don't know,' I said. 'Tell me.'

She drew the object slowly out, grinning wickedly at me as she waited for me to recognize it.

'It's a German stick grenade,' I said, with as calm a voice as I could muster. 'Anne, what are you going to do?'

'Do you know why it's called a stick grenade?' she asked, brandishing it. 'Because the stick attached to the grenade lets you throw it so much further, and I've been practicing. My best throw was twenty-seven feet.'

'Anne, what are you going to do?' I repeated.

'Kill as many limeys as I can before I leave town,' she said, shoving the grenade back into her pocketbook. 'I've got it all figured out. There's a bus stop outside the front of the library. I can wait for it at the door so no one notices me waiting on the street. I'll hop off at the British Embassy. Did you know those fools don't even have a wall around most of the embassy? I can just walk right up to the backside of the compound, where the offices are, and heave this grenade through a window into any room with lights on and people in it.'

'They'll catch you, and you'll hang for it!'

'No, they won't,' she said. 'I'll run south through the park until I get to Wisconsin Avenue. I can pick up a streetcar there and be on my way before the smoke clears at the embassy and the night watchman rousts the Royal Marines.'

She was right, she could pull it off.

'Tomorrow morning after the library opens you can tell the FBI and Lord Halifax, if he's alive, why I did it.'

'I'll tell them,' I said, desperate to know her entire story before she left, 'but I'll need some answers first.'

'More questions,' Anne said, sighing. 'You're determined, aren't you?'

'I just want to understand,' I said. 'I'm guessing Richard Martin was a Nazi agent?'

'Yes, he recruited me when he visited us before the war. The cousin thing was a complete invention. Leroy fell for it. He was not a bright man. I met Martin a couple of days later at a hotel in Annapolis, and he gave me the suitcase radio. I kept it under the bed, and Leroy never noticed it. Martin said that I'd get a postcard when I was needed. Then I was supposed to start monitoring the radio frequency he had me memorize for my instructions. The date was just one we settled on so that I'd know the postcard was authentic. Then you hand-delivered the postcard to me! And I started monitoring the frequency that very day.'

'You killed your husband,' I said.

She shrugged. 'I had to. He kept asking me why I lied about my birthday. And I couldn't figure out how to get him out of the house. Originally, the submarine was going to land the team on the eastern shore, on the Atlantic side. I was going to meet them and drive the saboteurs to Annapolis. But then the captain saw his chance to penetrate the Bay, and he couldn't resist it.'

'How did the Nazis know about you?'

'Between us my grandmother and I must have written a hundred letters, to the British, to the United Nations, to the Netherlands government, trying to get restitution from the British for the loss of our farm. The Germans found some of my letters in Hague after they conquered the Netherlands. You know how the Nazis love to riffle through other countries' file cabinets.' She glanced at her watch. 'That's enough now,' she said. 'Time to go.'

Anne kept the Luger at my back while she unlocked the staff entrance, which was in the rear of the library on the lower level. Once inside, the halls were dimly lit by a few random light fixtures, just enough to guide our way into the building. The back of the library held the book stacks and staff work rooms for cataloguing and such. The windows here were just slits, in case a bookshelf toppled. Of course, I'd never been in this part of the building.

With the rest of the public I spent my time on the first level, where the open, high-ceilinged reading rooms and the L'Enfant Map Room were located. But Anne knew her way around down here, and most of the way along the back hall she stopped in front of a door with 'bookbindery' lettered on it.

My heart began to pound. I didn't believe she intended to let me live. Anne opened the door and shoved me inside. I turned to face her, fully expecting her to shoot me. But, just as she had said, she spared me, closing the door on me. I heard the key turn in the lock. I was so relieved that my head spun and I sank to my knees on the cold marble floor while I listened to her footsteps recede.

Anne had said she would wait for the bus inside the library, near the front door. That meant she'd cross the building and climb the first flight of the Grand Staircase up to Literary Hall. From there she could station herself by one of the tall arched windows and watch for the bus. That would minimize her time standing in the street.

From there she'd go to the British Embassy to murder as many English men and women as she could. What a horrific scenario! Not just for the people who died, but for the United States government. Anne was an American citizen. Imagine the newspaper headlines in London!

Could I possibly escape this room and stop her?

I collected myself, felt for the edge of a table, and pulled myself up off the cold floor. It was pitch black. I found the door and turned the doorknob, not expecting success and not having any. Then I felt around the door until I found the light switch and flicked it on. Nothing happened, which I also expected. Most of the power to the building would be cut off to save electricity, except for a few lights scattered around the building.

Okay. This was the bookbindery. Could there be another entrance that Anne didn't know about? With an unlocked door? I doubted it, but I needed to find out. I felt my way around the perimeter of the room, running into bookshelves and tables that interrupted the walls as I went.

As I felt my way around one table I came across some tools of the bookbinders trade. A wooden press with an oversized screw, a sticky jar of glue, cardboard and leather rectangles, and then my fingers clasped an awl. It was about four inches long with a sharp point and a wooden handle that fit neatly into the palm of my hand. I slid it into my pea coat pocket. It wouldn't be much defense against a Luger but it was better than nothing.

The palms of my hands moved across empty wall again, until I came across a dumbwaiter. I knew that's what it was, there was no mistaking it. I felt around the edges. It was about four feet tall and a bit narrower, say three and a half feet. The door was divided horizontally with the two halves meeting in the middle. There were three buttons on a side panel. Lower Floor, First Floor, and Second Floor. I grabbed the door handle and pulled it down. Both halves of the door flew open with a loud clang. About halfway through the process an automatic function engaged and the door opened completely without any more leverage from me.

The dumbwaiter must be on a separate electric circuit from the lights.

The normal process for using the dumbwaiter was to close the doors and then select the floor. But I would need to do it backwards, pushing the button for the floor before pulling the door closed from inside. I didn't know if the dumbwaiter would even work with those two functions reversed.

My eyes had adjusted somewhat to the dark. Inside the dumbwaiter a shelf divided the space. I couldn't possibly fit inside. But when I grasped the shelf and pulled, it came out of the dumbwaiter and dropped on the floor with an echoing crash.

I climbed about halfway in before I felt panic hit. This was a tiny space. I'd have to fold myself into it to fit. How could I mash the button for the dumbwaiter to rise before the automatic door slammed on my arm? Would the dumbwaiter door rip my arm off if it was caught? Could I get the door open from inside? What if I was trapped inside until morning! I felt sweat begin to prickle between my shoulderblades.

I backed away from the dumbwaiter until I hit the edge of a table. I wasn't going up in that thing. It wasn't meant for people.

I completed my patrol around the edge of the bookbinding room. There were no other doors. I was stuck here.

Had Anne left the building yet? Even if she had, it was a long bus ride up to the British Embassy. There still might be time to stop her if I could get out of this room and find a telephone. Here in Washington I knew whom to call – the D.C. Metropolitan Police. Patrol cars were out on the streets all night, and they could get to the embassy quickly, find Anne and arrest her.

It was the dumbwaiter or nothing.

I didn't know until then that I was afraid of small dark enclosed places. Looking into the open dumbwaiter made me shudder with apprehension. I forced myself to climb inside, contorting myself into a position that left my hands free to work the controls of the dumbwaiter. Once inside I rehearsed. I was afraid I'd fracture a wrist if I didn't move decisively enough.

I stretched an arm around the front of the dumbwaiter and found the buttons by feel, since I wasn't about to poke my head out. I pushed the button for the first floor, then immediately grasped the top half of the door with both hands, gripping the edge with my palms facing toward me, and yanked the door down, drawing my hands inside as quickly as I could. Even then I felt the door graze my fingertips.

In the dark space I waited for the elevator to move, for what seemed like so long I thought its power was cut off too. Then, with a jerk, the dumbwaiter began to move upward. As I tried to calm my jangling nerves I told myself it would only be seconds until I reached the first floor, but then to my shock the dumbwaiter didn't stop! It kept climbing. I must have hit the wrong button. It didn't matter. I'd still be out of that coffin within minutes. Above me I heard the brake engage as the dumbwaiter stopped at the second floor of the library. Eagerly, I reached towards the door, only to find its surface completely flat, with just a crease to tell me where the halves met. I scrabbled at the crack in the door, trying to get enough purchase to force it open and up. The door didn't budge. I couldn't get out! How could I remain in this tiny space until morning and keep my sanity?

My chest heaved with apprehension, and I caught myself pummeling the metal door in frustration. The only thing that kept me from losing complete control was the thought that Anne might still be in the library and might hear me screaming and beating on the dumbwaiter door.

Working myself into a slightly more comfortable position, I curled up in a ball facing the door of the dumbwaiter. Here the staff of the library would find me tomorrow morning. How humiliating. I'd be the laughing stock of the entire city! I could just imagine the headlines. 'Failed would-be girl spy trapped in dumbwaiter overnight.' How mortifying.

Even worse, the British embassy would be counting its dead. Granted, Anne had a right to be angry, very angry, about British crimes during the Boer War. But that happened decades ago, and Lord Halifax and the men and women who worked at the British embassy today weren't responsible. Neither were the British people, who were suffering privations we couldn't imagine to keep Hitler at bay.

I shifted my position and felt something round and hard in my coat pocket. The awl I'd picked up in the bookbindery! I grabbed it and forced its blade into the crease between the two halves of the dumbwaiter door. Using the awl I pried the doors apart until I could grasp the edge of the top half and push it up. In the position I was in getting enough purchase seemed impossible at first, but then I put both feet up against the wall and shoved again.

The door flew open, and I tumbled out onto the marble floor, banging my knee in the process.

I didn't have time to recover. I had to find a telephone!

I was in the stacks surrounded by tall bookshelves, which loomed over me in the dark. I might have never found my way out, but a light on in a distant hall led me to a corridor lined with small offices. Telephones! The first door wasn't locked, but when I rushed for the telephone on the tiny desk there wasn't a dial tone.

The next office was locked.

The telephone was dead in the next office, too.

So the power to the telephone system must have been cut off when the electricity was shut off for the night. Maybe outside the building I could find a pay telephone that was working.

But I didn't have a key to the building!

At least I wasn't trapped in the dumbwaiter all night.

Then I remembered that on the first floor of the library, where the reading rooms were, there were two pay telephones, outside the L'Enfant Map Room. It was just possible they were on a different circuit than the library's telephones.

I followed the dim lights ahead of me, and after a short flight of marble stairs I found myself in a spacious foyer facing the Grand Staircase that led down to the first floor.

The staircase began its descent directly ahead, but shortly split in two, each half curving along the front wall of the library across the huge iron-framed windows that fronted the entrance of the building. The two staircases met at the small foyer inside the main door of the library. If Anne were still in the building she'd be waiting there for her bus.

My feet were sore and I needed to move quietly, so I had a momentary fanciful urge to slide down one of the winding mahogany bannisters, but figured I'd fly off at a curve and break my neck.

If one can tiptoe down a staircase, that's what I did, clinging to the bannister for support and stopping every few steps to listen. I heard only silence echoing. When I got near the bottom I sat down on a marble step and peered through the bannister railings. No one waited by the front door. I crept the rest of the way down, and then there was nothing else to do but step into the entrance foyer for a good look around. No one was there.

I felt relief course through my system, then remembered that what was good for me wasn't good for the British Embassy. If Anne had caught a bus shortly after locking me in the bindery, she would be most of the way there by now.

Two pay telephone booths stood across the wide hall next to the double doors of the L'Enfant Map Room. I ran across the marble floor, pulled open the mahogany door to one of the booths and grabbed for the telephone receiver. Thank you, Lord, a dial tone!

But I didn't have a nickel! Damn it, my pocket book was in Phoebe's car! Frantically, I searched through the pockets of the borrowed pea coat and trousers I was wearing. Not even a penny! I couldn't call the police. What now?

I heard a door slam nearby. Through the glass of the booth I saw Anne come out of a rest room across the foyer, her handbag clutched tightly to her side. She hadn't left yet after all. So there was still hope I could stop her.

Oh, she had a Luger, my switchblade, and a Nazi stick grenade, but I had a bookbinding awl, didn't I?

I slid onto the floor of the phone booth to hide and think.

Then I heard her footsteps. They were, step by step, inexorably coming my way! She must have seen me! And there I was, crouching on a telephone booth floor, so vulnerable. I was exhausted, and my feet were terribly sore. I was no match for her.

Anne would shoot me this time, I was sure of it.

As she came closer I could imagine her pulling the Luger out of her oversized pocketbook, her left hand reaching for the door of the box, and finally standing over me with her gun to my head.

Instead, I heard the door of the box next door open. Anne was making a telephone call! I squeezed tightly up against the wall next to her booth and strained to catch her words.

'Yes, yes,' she said. 'It's late. I've been waiting for almost an hour.'

She'd called the bus terminal!

'Are you sure it's running only ten minutes late? Yes, I know it's still icy in places. All right, of course I'll wait, I have no choice.'

I heard Anne hang up the telephone, and as she left the booth, I burst out of mine and tackled her from behind.

Taken completely by surprise, she landed flat on her stomach on the hard marble floor. I could hear her gasp as the air was knocked out of her lungs. Her pocketbook skidded across the floor, and I scrabbled over her to grab it.

Anne wasn't so easily defeated. She seized one of my sore feet with both hands, and I squealed in pain. She dragged me back towards her, and as I kicked back as hard as I could with my other foot she feinted backwards, letting go of me.

She was on her feet quickly, more quickly than I, and as I struggled to stand up to face her she slapped my face hard, knocking me to the side. I kept myself from falling flat by breaking my fall with my hands.

I rolled away just as she aimed a kick at my head.

If Anne hadn't missed that kick and lost her footing I'd be dead today, no question. It certainly wasn't skill that won me that fight. Anne lost her balance and toppled back against one of the telephone booths with one hand smashing back against the door.

I don't have a clear memory of what happened next, but the next thing I knew Anne was pinned to the door of the booth with a bookbinding awl piercing her hand. Blood trickled down her arm.

Anne didn't scream, but made soft moaning sounds while I went through her bag looking for the rope she used to tie me up in the car. When I found it I pulled the awl out of her twitching hand and tied her to a cast-iron grate in the wall. Blood gushed out of her wound, but I couldn't have cared less.

I found a nickel in her purse and called the police.

Anne hadn't gone meekly. She fought and screamed all the way to the paddy wagon. It took four policemen to force her inside and lock the door. I rode in another police car to the

DC Jail behind the paddy wagon. The jail was a famously hideous building, its plaster façade painted an odd blue to resemble stone, which it didn't at all.

Inside the stark police infirmary a medic cleaned and bandaged my feet and legs.

'Your lacerations and bruises aren't serious,' he said, 'but there are lots of them. You'll need to rest and stay off your feet for at least a week. I'll send some laudanum tablets home with you. You won't need them for more than a couple of days.'

I managed to nap for a couple of hours until Agent Williams showed up to debrief me. I told him the entire story, except for the part about how terrified I was of being trapped in the dumbwaiter.

'We caught the saboteurs,' Williams said. 'They were boarding a train for Chicago in Baltimore when one of them dropped the suitcase radio. It fell open on the platform, and the four of them were tackled by a bunch of GIs traveling in their car.'

The Navy and Coast Guard were scouring the bay for any sign of a scuttled Nazi submarine. If they located it they'd destroy it completely, so that the American public would never know that Germans had made their way into the Chesapeake Bay. Close watch was being kept on the coast of the eastern shore of Maryland, in hopes that the submariners could be captured trying to escape.

'Eastern Command gave us permission to search the Martin property yesterday mid-afternoon,' Williams said. 'While we were there Constable Long came driving like a maniac down the driveway. Some Coastguardsman had called him, wouldn't give him a name, crazy worried that he'd left you alone at the Martins. His HQ had forbidden him to report it, trying to keep the scene under wraps. Then Constable Long talked to Mrs Sullivan, who said Anne had called her and told her the two of you were together.'

Constable Long and Williams had searched for me, and Anne, in the vicinity of St Leonard for hours, until the DC police called them to tell them that Anne and I had been found.

'I suppose they'll charge her with treason?' I asked.

'I should think so. She's a citizen who aided an enemy of the United States, with intent to adhere to the enemy's cause.'

'Will she hang?'

'Nah. DC has an electric chair.'

EPILOG

I hobbled to the front door of 'Two Trees', with the support of a DC policeman on each arm.

Phoebe opened the door, and she and Ada rushed out into the cold to hug me.

'You poor girl!' Phoebe said.

'Louise, we've been so worried!' Ada said.

I winced as I moved to the door, and they both looked down at my bandaged legs and feet.

'Oh, my Lord!' Phoebe said.

'It's not as bad as it looks,' I said.

I thanked the policemen, one of whom had driven Phoebe's car home, miraculously without a scratch on it, and with Ada and Phoebe's help I limped inside the house.

'Baby,' Dellaphine said, standing in the hall with a tray holding a mug of hot cocoa and a plate of ham biscuits, 'what on earth happened to you?'

'I was walking on the beach after dark,' I said. 'It was so stupid of me. I tripped over a stone jetty and fell. I thought it would be smart to take off my shoes, to give me more traction, but then I stepped into a pile of oyster shells and fell again. I twisted my ankle and couldn't walk. I'd still be there, I think, if Mrs Sullivan hadn't called the local constable when I didn't return to her guesthouse.'

'Girls shouldn't be out walking any beach alone at night,' Henry said, coming out of the lounge.

Joe was behind him. I tried to read his expression and didn't see any anger there.

'Here,' he said, with a faint trill to the 'r', 'let me take you the rest of the way to the sofa.' He edged Ada and Phoebe aside, slid one arm under my shoulders and the other under my knees, and carried me into the warm lounge.

mL   1卜 /3